The Belly

by the same author

A ZED AND TWO NOUGHTS

The Belly of an Architect

PETER GREENAWAY

LONDON · BOSTON

First published in 1988
by Faber and Faber Limited
3 Queen Square London WC1N 3AU

Photoset and printed in Great Britain by
Redwood Burn Limited, Trowbridge, Wiltshire

British Library Cataloguing in Publication Data

Greenaway, Peter
The belly of an architect.
I. Title
822'.914 PR6057.R3/

ISBN 0-571-15080-2

Contents

Introduction

The Belly of an Architect is the contemporary story of a middle-aged American architect, Stourley Kracklite, who, with his young wife, Louisa, goes to Rome to set up an exhibition of the life and work of his hero, the eighteenth-century visionary architect, Etienne-Louis Boullée.

Stourley Kracklite and the Architecture of Rome are the film's two main characters in a story that takes nine months, a suitable gestation period to see Louisa from conception to birth and Kracklite from exultation to despair. Kracklite's obsessions and his selfishness antagonize his wife and his Roman hosts, and when frustration and illness begin to wear him down, the exhibition gradually slips out of his grasp. Kracklite's ambition to create visionary architecture just like his hero Boullée is mocked in Rome – as he knew it would be.

Eight of Rome's celebrated architectural sites chronologically structure *The Belly of an Architect*. They connect Boullée to Kracklite, for the first seven of them were Boullée's major inspiration; and they represent an architectural heritage of two and a half thousand years to put Kracklite's nine-month predicament into perspective. These buildings of so much architectural achievement underline the ephemerality of one foreign individual striving for significance in an eternal city that has absorbed so many foreigners.

The script presented here is predominantly the script presented to the producers for filming. Various forms of expediency that are always encountered in the making of a film – most importantly, the related factors of time and money – have intervened to force changes in the completed film. Some of the changes are regretted but many are welcomed. For me, the greatest casualty has been the loss of much dialogue, whilst the greatest benefit has been the excitement and visual splendour of the locations and the superb performance of Brian Dennehy as Stourley Kracklite.

PETER GREENAWAY
January 1987

Major Characters

STOURLEY KRACKLITE	A fifty-four-year-old American architect from Chicago. He is bearded and – initially at any rate – jocular. He has considerable physical presence.
LOUISA KRACKLITE	Stourley Kracklite's young wife – an American with Italian parents. She is twenty-seven, attractive and restless.
IO SPECKLER	Stourley Kracklite's host in Rome. In his early sixties, he too is an architect. He is an urbane and serious man with very courteous manners.
CASPASIAN SPECKLER	Io Speckler's son. Like his father and Kracklite, he is an architect. He is twenty-six, handsome, conceited, witty, malignant and ambitious.
FLAVIA SPECKLER	Io Speckler's daughter. She is a photographer. She is beautiful, sceptical, sharp-witted and sensual.
FREDERICO BOCCINI	Caspasian's friend. He is a talented model-maker, young, witty and mischievous.

The Belly of an Architect was released by Recorded Releasing and Palace Pictures and was first shown at the Gate cinema on 16 October 1987. The cast included:

STOURLEY KRACKLITE	Brian Dennehy
LOUISA KRACKLITE	Chloë Webb
CASPASIAN SPECKLER	Lambert Wilson
IO SPECKLER	Sergio Fantoni
FLAVIA SPECKLER	Stefania Cassini
FREDERICO BOCCINI	Vanni Corbellini
Director of Photography	Sacha Vierny
Art Director	Luciana Vedovelli
Costume Designer	Maurizio Millenotti
Editor	John Wilson
Music	Wim Mertens
Additional Music	Glenn Branca
Producers	Colin Callender and Walter Donohue
Writer/Director	Peter Greenaway

Section One: Soon after Dawn on Friday, 24 May 1985

SCENE 1: THE RAILWAY LINE FROM VENTIMIGLIA

A railway train rushes through a Mediterranean landscape soon after dawn . . . past farms and fields of olive trees lit by the low early-morning sun. The landscape is viewed at speed through the window of one of the train's sleeping compartments where a man and a woman – oblivious to the passing countryside – make love. The train passes close to the walls of a modest country cemetery – a graveyard where rusting iron crosses and faded porcelain photographs are lit and crossed with the sunlight and shadow of the early-morning sun. This is the first and most modest reference to all the many architectural monuments to death that are to come.

As the couple in the sleeping compartment continue to make love, the train approaches the country suburbs of a small town . . . the town of Ventimiglia, official crossing-point from France into Italy.

SCENE 2: VENTIMIGLIA STATION

On Friday, 24 May 1985, at Ventimiglia, the train draws into Platform 3 in the early-morning light.

Across the tracks, seven passengers are standing patiently on Platform 2 – two men and two women, a priest, a child and a violinist who carries a worn, crimson violin-case.

Along the platform are several identical travel posters advertising Rome – they show the Roman she-wolf suckling her human twins, Romulus and Remus.

The name of the station, 'Ventimiglia', rings out several times in a sing-song manner over the station loudspeaker.

The train windows slowly flick by – each one catching the brilliant warm orange light of the morning sun. The train comes to a slow halt.

Sunlight and shadows from the station buildings criss-cross the train; water drips from a drain-pipe. There is the sound of muted distant carriage conversation.

At the window of the carriage that stops immediately opposite the platform passengers, the window blind – three-quarters drawn –

is moving up and down with a regular movement. Two shadowy figures move behind it. The passengers on the platform draw the conclusion that the two people in the carriage are probably absorbed in a less than ambiguous occupation.
There is the distant clink of bottles, a distant train whistle. Eventually – but still with some ambiguity in the shadows – a man's naked backside is seen between the window blind and the bottom of the window frame. The station passengers watch. They look at one another to confirm the evidence of their eyes. If they have an opinion on the matter, it is not apparent in their faces. With the passengers still watching, the train begins to move out of the station.

SCENE 3: INSIDE THE TRAIN COMPARTMENT
In the deep shadow of the carriage compartment of the moving train, a man and a woman finish making love and part.
It is still early morning. A thin strip of light coming into the compartment from beneath the window blind is the sole source of illumination, which is enough to see that the man is aged about fifty-four and the woman is aged around twenty-six: STOURLEY KRACKLITE and LOUISA KRACKLITE, husband and wife. She is attractive and voluptuous – though beside her husband she looks small. He is a large man – powerfully built – and luxuriantly bearded.
Through the thin strip at the bottom of the blind is an orange, dawn-lit, North Italian landscape. The light flickers – interrupted by poles and posts and trees and the dark shapes of buildings. The man and the woman lie on their backs among the bed sheets; their stomachs parallel, one behind the other as the Italian early-morning sunlit landscape passes by outside of the train window. The woman is tanned – she obviously likes sun-bathing. The man is whiter skinned – he is not over-excited at spending long hours lying in the sun. Both of them now lie in luxurious exhaustion. Stripes of sunlight repeatedly flick across their bodies. The silhouetted profiles of their faces are barely seen.
LOUISA stretches and sits up and, lifting the window blind a few inches, peers out into the sunlight which backlights her arms as

she fastens her brassière. She laughs.

LOUISA: What a way to enter Italy!

KRACKLITE: (*Feeling expansive after love-making*) On the contrary – the ideal way. Land of fertility . . . fine women . . . inimitable history . . . home of the dome and the arch . . . (*Self-mockingly he makes the shape of the dome and the arch across his belly*) . . . and good food . . . (*Pats his belly*) . . . and high ideals (*Raises his hands in the air*).

LOUISA: (*Scornfully and playfully*) *My* father was Italian. *He* wasn't fat – he was thin . . .

KRACKLITE: (*Smiling*) But carnivorous enough!

LOUISA: (*As she looks out of the carriage window at the passing landscape*) . . . he was only interested in money . . . and he had no ideals except to leave the place.

KRACKLITE: He was bright enough to take his money to Chicago . . .

LOUISA: City of blood, meat and money . . .

KRACKLITE: (*With a laugh*) Home of the best carnivorous architecture in the Western World . . . that is, (*Begrudgingly, and with a smile*) of course, outside of Rome . . .

Section Two: Late Afternoon on Friday, 24 May 1985

SCENE 4: ENTRY INTO ROME

Exultant, massive, grand, rhythmic chords introduce the title of the film and the subsequent major credits which are superimposed over a montage of Rome's architecture as seen from a moving vehicle.

The buildings loom and pass with a rhythmic regularity – shining cupolas, dark domes, shadowy arches, artificially lit statuary, white marble, green verdigris roofing, warm brickwork, black voids, eroded architraves, statues of elderly men, sensuous odalisques wet with fountain water, silhouetted pillars – an unashamed celebration of the Rome architectural heritage. There are several choicely placed references to meat, blood, money and slaughter: the sun's red glow on a statue of disembowellment, on a graphic crucifixion, a glimpse of a butcher's well-stocked shop window, an ornate bank.

As this sequence progresses, the images get darker and darker, until only fleeting and ambiguous architectural details are visible. The music assumes more and more 'architectural' power.

SCENE 5: THE ROME APARTMENT

With the last sequence continuing in half-glimpsed images and loud celebratory music, the KRACKLITES have arrived at the gloomy echoic spaces of a grand Roman house and are being conducted to their suite of rooms. There is now heard the jangling of heavy keys, the murmur of distant conversations, calls in Italian, the echoic footfalls on marble floors.

Occasional glimpses into rich, shadowy patio gardens and details of rich architectural mouldings, door-jambs, friezes, ceilings are seen in ever-growing darkness.

This darkness is suddenly shattered by double shutters being thrown open to reveal the sunset over the Mausoleum of Augustus – the sky is a mass of swirling starlings. The music stops. The eyes are stunned. The ears are left ringing in the intrusive silence.

LOUISA: My God – what's that?

KRACKLITE: (*With awe and delight*) The Tomb of Augustus!

The view of the Tomb of Augustus is held in a static frame – a finely composed shot – balancing the sunset and the local artificial street-lighting – making an 'architectural' shot of great power – giving the formally defined building great presence.

The porter who carried the bags waits impatiently for a tip – KRACKLITE gives him a note – he looks displeased – KRACKLITE gives him a second note. LOUISA flops down on to the large and luxurious double bed – she looks very attractive and sensuous in her crumpled travelling clothes. KRACKLITE turns back to the view through the window.

Time-lapse 1

There now follows the first of eight shots that make a formal record of the eight Roman buildings or groups of buildings – mostly tombs or memorials – that influenced Boullée, or, ironically, in the last case, that Boullée influenced. They are: the Mausoleum of Augustus, the Pantheon, the Colosseum, the Baths

of the Villa Adriana, the Piazza and Dome of St Peter's, the Forum, the Piazza Navona and the EUR Building.
The ambition of using these shots – each some 15–25 seconds long (maybe longer) – is to find a powerful visual metaphor for Rome's age and endurance, its architecture seemingly independent of the activities and time scale of man. Each of the eight shots is to be constructed in such a way that exaggerated (universal) time – i.e. the slow curve of the sun from noon, through the afternoon into sunset and night over the Colosseum, condensed into some 30 seconds – should imperceptibly convert to real time (and by inference ephemeral time) where a character in the film is perceived to being going about his second-by-second mundane business.
These shots are accompanied by 'grand', even 'grandiose', exultant music that comments on the power of Rome, Roman architecture and Roman history, and on Time itself.

In this instance of the time-lapse, as KRACKLITE looks on, the May sun sinks down behind the Tomb of Augustus, the sky quickly grows redder and redder, the last clouds of the day move rapidly across the sky, artificial lights flick on, night descends, the Mausoleum is floodlit. Converting down from exaggerated time to real time, with the music dying away to accentuate the 'return to normality', the camera pulls back to reveal KRACKLITE at the open window. He turns to face into the room to look at his wife drowsing on the bed. Lying invitingly, she makes the view out of the window even more poignant – she suggests the sensuous exhaustion of death. KRACKLITE senses it and is much attracted to it. He sits on the bed beside her, then kneels, puts his hand on her leg under her skirt, and travels his hand up her leg to her thigh. She doesn't move. He buries his face in her lap. She stirs and opens her eyes.

LOUISA: I'm hungry, Kracklite.

KRACKLITE: (*Muffled*) Let's eat . . .

LOUISA: . . . and I'm thirsty.

KRACKLITE: Let's drink. (*He has raised his head*) I'll call room service.

(*He reaches out a hand for the phone beside the bed.*)

LOUISA: No Stourley! I want to eat in public . . . You can't eat alone in Rome . . . Italians don't eat alone!

KRACKLITE: (*Sounding piqued*) Is being with me 'alone'?

LOUISA: (*Getting up and switching on the two bedside lamps*) No . . . Kracklite (*Affectionately ironic*) – being with you is like being with a circus. (*She brushes him a peremptory kiss as she gets up taking off her coat.*) Get dressed – we're eating out – we're expected.

While LOUISA unfastens her suitcases, KRACKLITE throws off his shoes, slips off his jacket and jumps on to the bed, lifting his large suitcase with him. The weight of the suitcase makes his face red – he stands awkwardly – quite likely to strain his stomach muscles. In one baroque gesture – causing him to grunt with the effort – he both opens the suitcase and upends it. The contents – mainly books and brightly coloured ties – scatter everywhere. They bounce on the bed and fall on to the floor. LOUISA looks up in disgust and annoyance.

LOUISA: God!

The books continue to bounce and slither. They are all expensive-looking, hard-cover books on architecture and related subjects – many of them feature the name or the works of the French architect Etienne-Louis Boullée. The bookjackets indicate Boullée's period, nationality, dates and profession: late eighteenth-century, neo-classical, French, 1728–1799, visionary architect.

Montage

This fall of books is the cue for a celebratory montage – cut to exultant music – of Boullée's contribution to visionary architecture – black-and-white and sepia drawings, plans and designs of opera houses, libraries, grandiose palaces of justice, city gates, public baths, high spiralling towers, ideal cities on vast plains, monumental cenotaphs and immense memorials. Rapidly following one another, this sequence of drawings and plans finishes with a wide aspect of the memorial Boullée designed for Sir Isaac Newton . . . a building inspired by the Rome Pantheon about to appear in the next scene.

Section Three: Approaching Midnight on Friday, 24 May 1985

SCENE 6: THE PANTHEON RESTAURANT

A wide shot of the flood-lit Pantheon. It's held for 10 seconds and accompanied by exultant music. It is a warm, late May evening. The massive bulk of the Pantheon is picked out in white floodlighting, areas of pitch black and more local areas of yellow street-lighting. The whole effect is theatrical, massive and signals age and power . . . and some threat. The camera slowly retreats from the façade to reveal, dwarfed by the Pantheon, the chairs, tables and awnings of a candlelit supper party laid outside the terrace of an expensive restaurant. Eight people – the men in dark suits – are celebrating around a table that indicates the meal is well into the dessert course. Flowers, glasses, napkins, fruit, figs, cutlery cover the table.

The guests are: STOURLEY KRACKLITE – wearing a black suit with a red silk shirt and a red silk tie – looking a little like a Prohibition gangster; LOUISA KRACKLITE – dressed in a low-cut white evening dress; IO SPECKLER, the host, and architect responsible for the Kracklites' presence in Rome. He is in his early sixties – some twelve years older than KRACKLITE – an urbane, serious man with greying hair and extremely courteous manners. He is very knowledgeable, with his scepticism more English than Italian; CASPASIAN SPECKLER, IO's son – also an architect – twenty-five, handsome, conceited, witty, malignant and ambitious – scrupulously and expensively dressed; FLAVIA SPECKLER, IO's daughter – a photographer specializing in sculpture, architecture and painting – beautiful in an eccentric way – as in a Mannerist painting – small head, long neck and athletic body . . . stylish clothes – dangerous, sensuous, witty and sharp.

These are the important figures. Those that follow are supporting cast . . .

JULIO FICCONE, gallery curator – an elderly man – a scholar – somewhat dry, fastidious, patriotic – the contemporary of Io Speckler; FREDERICO BOCCINI, CASPASIAN's friend – a young man, an experienced and talented model-maker. He is witty and

flippant – bleeds easily – somewhat childish and unpredictable – easily led. He wears a dark blue suit and a crimson tie; CLAUDIA BORROMINO – FLAVIA's friend – a beautiful thirty-year-old blonde – it's not certain whether she is, or is not, stupid.
Swagged across one end of the room is a silk banner with the inscription 1728–1799 ETIENNE-LOUIS BOULLÉE.
It is KRACKLITE's fifty-fourth birthday. A large, iced cake, carried on a trestle, is brought to the table by two waiters. The cake is fashioned in the shape of a building – the prime building of the French architect Etienne-Louis Boullée – the memorial building dedicated to Isaac Newton. The cake has fifty-four candles arranged around the circumference of the dome. The cake is placed in front of KRACKLITE who looks surprised, delighted and moved.
The guests clap. KRACKLITE gets to his feet. With the artificially lit domed Pantheon behind him and the artificially lit domed model of the Newton building on the table in front of him, he makes a speech. He starts very formally, and a little pompously.

KRACKLITE: Friends – I propose a toast to Etienne-Louis Boullée whose designs were – and are – an inspiration to thousands of architects, but – alas – whose completed buildings can be counted on the fingers of one hand. (*Holds up five fingers.*) Etienne-Louis Boullée died 186 years ago and there has been no major showing of his work anywhere in the world. I am grateful that you are now to be the hosts of an extraordinary and comprehensive exhibition of his life and work which I am convinced will help to redress the balance of his obscurity. I am especially grateful to Signor Speckler (*Indicating him*) for inviting me to come and mount this exhibition here, in Rome – city of Boullée's major inspiration, and cradle of all Western architecture. (*Turning his attention to the cake*) Boullée's crowning achievement – inspired by the magnificent building of the Pantheon behind us (*He indicates the Pantheon*) – was the memorial he designed to Sir Isaac Newton – the Einstein of his day. (*Pointing to the cake*) I doubt whether Sir Isaac Newton has previously been celebrated in icing sugar. (*There is laughter – and* KRACKLITE, *with an outstretched finger, touches the smooth, white, icing-sugar dome.*)

. . . for me, after waiting so very long to honour a visionary architect I have passionately admired ever since I was a child . . . this moment is very sweet indeed.
(*He licks his finger – there is laughter and* KRACKLITE *raises his glass.*)
. . . to Etienne-Louis Boullée!

Everyone around the table follows suit and toasts Boullée, FLAVIA SPECKLER takes flash photographs, LOUISA kisses her husband on the cheek and there are shouts of 'Happy Birthday'. The waiters clap.

KRACKLITE: Now – although it is *my* birthday, if you will permit it, I would like to call on my wife to cut this magnificent cake (*With good humour*) – she is excellent at opening events, kissing babies, naming ships, planting trees – cutting the tape.
(*There is laughter and clapping as* LOUISA *stands up.*)

LOUISA: (*With a wry look at her husband*) I have opened more buildings than I care to admit.
(*Laughter.*)
Though not enough of them have been my husband's.
(*Laughter.*) I couldn't think of spoiling such a beautiful cake.
(*Looking at* FREDERICO) How long did it take you to make it?

FREDERICO: (*Replying with an ironic sparkle*) Considerably less, I imagine, that it took Boullée to design the original . . . about the same time perhaps that it took Sir Isaac Newton to recover from the apple falling on his head.
(*He thumps the top of his head – there is laughter.*)

CLAUDIA: Then did it kill him?

FREDERICO: (*Laughing*) No – as with Adam – an apple made him famous.

FLAVIA: . . . making them both free from constipation.
(*Laughter.*)

CLAUDIA: Eh?

FLAVIA: The English have an expression, 'An apple a day keeps the doctor away' – isn't that so, Kracklite?
(*She looks significantly at him.*)

CASPASIAN: (*Dismissively*) All English architects are constipated.

There is a white silk ribbon swagged around the cake with the words, 'Etienne-Louis Boullée 1728–1799' printed on it. While the conversation around the table continues, LOUISA is handed a shiny pair of silver scissors by FREDERICO.

LOUISA – with panache – cuts the tape. It falls away to either side (a gesture and action exactly – and ironically in the circumstances – repeated at the ceremony at the end of the film). There is clapping and cheering. FLAVIA takes photographs – very professionally. A waiter hands LOUISA a sharp and shiny cake knife that glistens in the candlelight. The waiters dim all the electric lights as LOUISA hesitates to cut into the large, smooth, 'pregnant' dome of the cake's architectural decoration.

CASPASIAN, with a great show of politeness, offers to help. He takes her hand in his and together they cut the cake. The sharp knife slices into the smooth, glistening sphere . . . the cake crumples and buckles along the knife-edge. There is a commiserating cry mingled with a cheer from the guests whose faces are lit up by the candles that are still burning on the cake. FLAVIA rapidly takes photographs of LOUISA and KRACKLITE. Beyond and behind the guests, the perfect dome of the Pantheon dominates the setting – standing firm while the cake-dome crumples. KRACKLITE – watching – looks slightly disconcerted . . . at LOUISA behaving so coquettishly with CASPASIAN, at the carefully constructed cake-model being destroyed, and – perhaps more fully than most around the table – finding the gesture a disturbing metaphor. He breaks his own reverie to draw the guests' attention back to himself.

KRACKLITE: In England, architects are respected. Sir Christopher Wren, complete with his portrait, buildings and plans, appears on the English fifty-pound note – architects are expensive –

(*Laughter.*)

– but . . . Sir Isaac Newton, the subject of this cake, is in every Englishman's wallet . . . he's on the English one-pound note. (*Looking in his wallet*) I always carry one on me for good luck. A man who discovered gravity and thus successfully secured our feet on the ground is a good companion.

(*Clapping and laughter.*)

(*Continuing – developing his metaphor*) In fixing us to the earth,

he enabled us – with equanimity – to permit our heads to remain in the clouds . . .
(*The clapping and laughter is exaggeratedly enthusiastic.*)
If you look at an English pound note . . .
(*He takes out the note and shows it to* CLAUDIA *and* FLAVIA *who are sitting nearest to him – they all three bend over the note in the candlelight.*)
. . . you will see the reference to gravity – can you spot it?
(*They point to the diagram on the note.*)
No!
(*Then they point to the book on Newton's lap.*)
No!

A slice is lifted from the cake – complete with its candles – and put on a small plate – it is handed towards LOUISA. The knife is given to a waiter who continues to cut slices – the splendid cake diminishes – it looks like a ruined, gutted building on fire. The cake, the currency note, and the close-ups of the women's faces – all add up to a complex metaphor of money and destruction – all seen in the flickering candlelight. Behind it all, the Pantheon stands immutable.

KRACKLITE: It's an *English* banknote and therefore much more laconic – you'll have to look harder. (*Points to the note*) It's here – look! – the apple-blossom!

The pound note is passed around the table for inspection. KRACKLITE forgets it, occupied by other matters . . . namely CASPASIAN's eyes for LOUISA.

FLAVIA: (*Passing* KRACKLITE *a large slice*) Here is your slice of the cake, (*Ironically*) *Mr* Kracklite . . . are architects in the habit of eating buildings?

KRACKLITE: If they have the appetite for them.
(*He sinks his teeth in.*)

LOUISA: And the gut to digest them.
(*She fondly pats her husband's stomach below the belt, amid laughter.*)

CASPASIAN: (*With ironic intent*) Was Boullée a large man, Mr Kracklite?

KRACKLITE: (*Through mouthfuls of cake, but with equal irony*) Not especially, Signor Speckler – five foot seven and twelve stone . . .

FLAVIA: (*She looks at* LOUISA) Was Boullée married?
KRACKLITE: (*Looking at his wife*) Certainly not to a butcher's daughter.
CLAUDIA: (*Looking at* LOUISA *and smiling*) Is that true?
(LOUISA *is eating the cake with relish – there are crumbs on her chin.* CASPASIAN *smiles and watches with interest.*)
LOUISA: My father made his money exporting meat – as sausages.
JULIO: (*Incredulously*) You built the Chicago–Angelo Building entirely on the profit from sausages?
KRACKLITE: (*Laughing*) And a little minced meat . . . chitterlings . . . frankfurters . . . salami . . . pork pies . . .
(*He is now eating figs.*)
CASPASIAN: (*Dismissively*) A veritable monument to carnivores!
LOUISA: (*Mockingly*) In Chicago, they call it the Charnel House. A building suffering from excess cholesterol . . . like Stourley.
KRACKLITE: (*A trifle put out*) There is no fat on it – or me . . . (*Self-mockingly, and putting a peeled fig in his mouth*) It's just that both of us *are* built with a perfect and enviable centre of gravity.
(*Laughter* – LOUISA, *having heard the joke many times before, grimaces.*)
FLAVIA: Standing up?
LOUISA: No, Signora Speckler – (*Disparagingly*) lying down!
(*There is laughter, and a special significant exchange of glances between* LOUISA *and* FLAVIA.)

FLAVIA continues to take photos of LOUISA and KRACKLITE. The party, in ones and twos, gets up from the table and drifts towards the Pantheon. KRACKLITE is still eating figs – he carries a supply of them in a table napkin. There is fig juice on his chin. CLAUDIA – perhaps a little coquettishly – wipes it off for him. IO carries a glass of brandy, CASPASIAN smokes a cigarette, FREDERICO has his hands in his pocket, LOUISA and FLAVIA carry wine glasses.
They congregate at the fountain in the middle of the piazza. The Pantheon looms over them – lit both with floodlights and street

lamps – but also presenting great areas of gloom and black voids. The rippling light reflected from the fountain basin, shimmers over the diners.

KRACKLITE: I used to dream about the Pantheon – it worried me. It should have been covered in marble – where's all the marble gone? It's got an open roof – what happens when it rains? Is it true they kept horses in it?

IO: The buildings in Rome are so old – there is no purpose to which each has not been put. (*Provocatively*) I wonder if such a recommendation could be claimed for contemporary architecture?

FREDERICO: Is it true, Signor Kracklite, that *you* designed a monument to a horse?

KRACKLITE: (*Pleased to be asked*) To a horse *and* its rider . . . a lady.

LOUISA: (*Looking significantly at* KRACKLITE) . . . a lady whose moral outlook was long past rescue.

KRACKLITE: (*Eating his way through his figs*) A few days before it was finished – horse and rider got struck by lightning. So the stable was locked up as a permanent memorial.

LOUISA: (*Witheringly*) To the neighbours – it was yet another empty garage.

(*She links her arm into* FLAVIA's.)

IO: (*Laughing*) There *is* a Roman proverb that involves horses and this building.

(*He points to the Pantheon and declaims the Latin proverb – they are standing near the entrance – and his voice echoes under the columns.*)

Poorly translated, it means 'Who comes to Rome and never sees the Pantheon leaves and returns an ass.'

They all laugh and the laughter echoes around the building. Smiling, FLAVIA takes photographs, and then, leading LOUISA by the arm, the two of them stroll back to the restaurant, leaving the others talking.

Seen from behind the restaurant table, LOUISA and FLAVIA approach, their arms linked . . . they drink from the same glass – a conspiratorial relationship already developed between them. They enter the restaurant (soon to appear on the restaurant balcony). KRACKLITE and his party amble in front of the Pantheon – their long shadows are thrown across the flagstones. Their conversation is heard across the space between them and the restaurant. There is talk of a race. CLAUDIA grabs KRACKLITE's hand and, pulling him, urges him to run.

CLAUDIA: Come on, Signor Kracklite! You must join in the race too. Just a few steps will do! They say it's lucky for fathers who want sons to run round the Pantheon! (*Laughs and pulls on his arm.*) Although you are a large man, Signor Kracklite, it is still bigger than you are – you must pay homage.

After being about to run to please CLAUDIA, KRACKLITE stops and feels in all his jacket pockets.

CLAUDIA: What have you lost?

KRACKLITE: (*In some real distress*) My pound note – my good luck token!

CLAUDIA: (*Pulling him along*) Come on – you can easily get another.

KRACKLITE: You can't. They are dropping out of circulation.

CLAUDIA: (*Laughing merrily*) So much for Sir Isaac Newton and gravity!

Up on the restaurant balcony, LOUISA and FLAVIA emerge to lean on the balcony rail and watch the activity in the square below them.

FLAVIA: (*Nodding at* KRACKLITE *in the piazza*) How long have you been married to him?

LOUISA: Seven years. (*Laughing ironically*) Do you think that's too long? I was twenty when we met. He was forty-seven.

FLAVIA: God! (*Raised eyebrows*) Did your parents approve?

From the balcony, FLAVIA photographs the people in the square. The camera now begins a long slow vertical fall. It moves down past a Latin inscription, down to the street level where the waiters are clearing away the remains of the dinner. The collapsed ruin of the model-cake lies illuminated by its guttering candles. Kracklite's English pound note, smeared with marzipan, is among the ruins. At Io's vacated place, there is a large wad of Italian banknotes stuffed under a plate. The waiters clear the table, pocket the money. The English pound note is picked out by a waiter and scrupulously cleaned – even licked clean – before being pocketed. The camera watches all this while we listen to the conversation between LOUISA and FLAVIA.

LOUISA: My mother did. And I *always* liked what she liked. (*Sighing a little bitterly*) I can't say the same any more.
(FLAVIA *smiles and raises her eyebrows questioningly* – LOUISA *shrugs and continues flippantly*.)
My father always wanted me to marry an Italian (*Laughs*) – so that I would know my place. He wanted hundreds of little Itie grandchildren . . . he took me to the opera, he paid for Italian lessons. He sang *Pagliacci* in the bathroom . . .

FLAVIA: (*Dismissively and humorously*) All Italians do that.

The camera, having watched the activities of the restaurant on the street level, now begins a vertical climb back up to the balcony and FLAVIA and LOUISA.

LOUISA: Kracklite was a respected Chicago architect – he often had his name in the papers – he travelled in Europe a great deal . . . teaching, lecturing . . . My father wouldn't consider an Italian architect to build him a prestige building – he was sure they would all cheat him . . . so, not without a little persuasion from my mother – Kracklite got the job . . .

FLAVIA: (*Laughing*) I can see he would be good with elderly ladies.

FLAVIA takes photos of LOUISA on the balcony – LOUISA is not displeased to be photographed.

In front of the Pantheon, CASPASIAN, FREDERICO, CLAUDIA and KRACKLITE are ready for a race around the Pantheon. CASPASIAN carefully takes off his double-breasted jacket, watched by KRACKLITE with some distaste for his over-zealous concern with his clothes. CASPASIAN folds the jacket neatly and gives it to his father to hold. His father negligently arranges it over his own shoulders.

'Ready steady go!' is shouted in Italian and, accompanied by exultant music, they set off. CASPASIAN and FREDERICO in real competition, CLAUDIA pushing KRACKLITE. Their laughter and footsteps echo in the empty streets.

The race is watched by LOUISA and FLAVIA, who continue their conversation on the restaurant balcony.

LOUISA: Kracklite talked endlessly to my father about Italy

. . . about Rome . . . its buildings, its monuments, its contribution to the American way of life . . . He ate my mother's Italian cooking like a starving schoolboy . . . They were won over . . . the building was a fashionable success, Kracklite became celebrated . . . I was young . . . I was impressed . . . my father's wedding present was another commission for Kracklite – to build us a house – you should see it! – two cubes and a sphere on stilts – Boullée would have loved it . . . (*A long sad pause.*) However . . . my father has had to wait a long time for his grandchildren . . . (*Shrugging and laughing*) . . . even the American ones.

FLAVIA looks at her curiously – smiles with her – kisses her on the cheek – and takes a photograph of her.

The distance around the Pantheon is about 400 yards – it's an island of masonry surrounded by the square on one side and three narrow streets on the other three sides.

FREDERICO and CASPASIAN are well out in front, running in the white light of a street lamp – their shadows stretched out on the paving stones behind them. KRACKLITE – some one hundred yards behind them – is running a little in front of the laughing CLAUDIA, hobbling in her high heels.

IO and JULIO are still standing in front of the Pantheon. Behind them a waiter is carrying two café chairs to the front of the Pantheon.

With the camera running both behind and alongside them – CASPASIAN and FREDERICO half shout, half talk – their figures and shadows making great play with the various sources of artificial light.

CASPASIAN: What do you think of our foreign architect?

FREDERICO: He's too old for his wife!

CASPASIAN: She's obviously looking for a 'Romantic Experience'.

FREDERICO: How can you tell?

CASPASIAN: The way she eats cake!

FREDERICO: The way she eats cake?

CASPASIAN: Yes – all tongue and crumbs. Beat you to the front!

They sprint with CASPASIAN in the lead. FREDERICO stumbles

and crashes to the floor. He picks himself up – bleeding from the cheek, and from the wrist. CASPASIAN sees FREDERICO's plight, but doesn't stop – he runs backwards, laughing. FREDERICO's hand and cheek are gashed and bloody. He looks piqued and upset like a child.

Out of sight of the other runners, the second pair, KRACKLITE and CLAUDIA, are rounding a corner – illuminated by an orange street light – their shadows are thrown tall on the stonework of an ancient house. KRACKLITE – puffing with the exertion and some twenty paces ahead – rounds the corner and – out of view of CLAUDIA – suddenly doubles up clutching his stomach. In pain he stumbles to the nearest supporting wall and leans against it – his head buried under his arm.

Hearing a mingled cry of anger and surprise – followed by a laugh – he looks behind him to see CLAUDIA has tripped and lost the heel of one of her high-heeled shoes. KRACKLITE flattens himself against the wall until the pain goes, his face relaxes and he swallows hard. He then slowly goes back to assist CLAUDIA.

At the front of the Pantheon – under the huge letters of the pediment – there are two chairs placed fronting the Pantheon. A waiter approaches with two more. IO and JULIO sit contemplating the façade and quietly talking to one another. CASPASIAN and FREDERICO come running around the corner back to where they started. CASPASIAN is running full tilt – FREDERICO no more than jogging. IO and CASPASIAN sit FREDERICO on a chair and examine FREDERICO's face. IO sends a waiter back to the restaurant for some water. The other waiter approaches with more chairs – which he arranges in a line with the others. There are now seven chairs in the line.

Meanwhile KRACKLITE has arrived – looking very grey and heavily sweating – supporting CLAUDIA who is carrying her shoes and walking barefoot. The waiter hurries over with a cloth and a bowl of warm water. All minister to FREDERICO – which is ironic – it should be KRACKLITE who they minister to – FREDERICO is always treated like a baby. He is good-looking in a childish way. People like to fuss and touch him.

FLAVIA and LOUISA arrive. CASPASIAN takes his jacket from his father and carefully puts it on. Eventually all seven are seated on the chairs in a line. The camera travels along them – FREDERICO, with a white face, mops his bloody cheek, CLAUDIA hugs her high-heeled shoes (her feet are bare), CASPASIAN has his arm along the back of LOUISA's chair, KRACKLITE is stiff with anticipated pain, IO looks excited, FLAVIA amused, JULIO thoughtful.

IO: (*Looking at his watch*) Just about this time – if I'm in the neighbourhood – I come and applaud such a great work of architecture (*Rhapsodizes*) – as wide as it is tall – as solid as it is beautiful – as romantic as it is awesome – built by Hadrian – most accomplished of all the Emperors!

As he speaks, at least six sets of bells in the neighbourhood irregularly strike midnight. As they ring, IO starts to clap.

IO: (*Excited, raising his voice above the sound of the bells*) Good architecture should always be applauded!

All the others, seated on the line of chairs as though in a row at the theatre – begin to clap. CLAUDIA gleefully, FLAVIA ironically, LOUISA self-consciously. They applaud the Pantheon . . . enthusiastically . . .

The music – in the background since the end of the race around the Pantheon – now thunders back in – taking its cue from the volume and insistence of the bells, to accompany:

Time-lapse 2

The camera – from a position behind the applauding admirers – slowly tilts up to clear their heads and present a wide-screen finely composed view of the Pantheon and the night sky above and behind. Imperceptibly, real time goes into exaggerated time and we watch the moon steadily rise and sail in an arc over the Pantheon . . .

Section Four: The Night of Saturday, 25 May 1985

SCENE 7: FIRST ILLNESS IN THE APARTMENT

In the apartment suite at night – KRACKLITE and LOUISA have returned from the evening meal. LOUISA is farther advanced at undressing – she is putting on her nightgown . . . KRACKLITE is still in his jacket – he's leaning out of the window looking at the Mausoleum of Augustus.

KRACKLITE: (*Sardonically*) I notice that Caspasian wears a double-breasted suit . . .
(*He takes off his jacket and throws it across the room on to a chair.*)
LOUISA: (*Getting into bed*) So?
KRACKLITE: . . . that he wears matching tie-pin and cuff-links (*Snags his tie while attempting to take it off and finally lifts it off over his head*) . . . that he wears a ring – and I shouldn't be surprised – a medallion around his neck. (*He empties his trouser pockets of loose change, keys, pens and a wallet and arranges them scrupulously on the glass top of the dressing table – a gesture reprised later.*)
LOUISA: (*Amused and feeding his jealousy*) Do you want me to find out?
KRACKLITE: (*Taking off his shirt*) Would you *want* to find out?
LOUISA: (*A little bored*) It's not important.
KRACKLITE: What *is* important?
LOUISA: To ingratiate yourself with the Specklers – they have influence.
KRACKLITE: And charm.
(*He sits on the bed to take off his shoes.*)
LOUISA: Don't they?
KRACKLITE: Caspasian especially.
(*He throws one of his shoes across the room.*)
LOUISA: (*With a smile*) Especially . . . Are you jealous?
KRACKLITE: Of charm – no. (*Throws his other shoe after the first.*) Of medallions – certainly not. (*Takes off a sock.*) Of his youth – possibly.
(*He takes off his other sock and throws them after his shoes.*)
LOUISA: Of his ability as an architect?
KRACKLITE: (*Quickly*) Least of all – he seems talentless.
LOUISA: Oh–ah!
KRACKLITE: What does 'oh–ah!' mean?
(*He suddenly grimaces and holds his stomach –* LOUISA *doesn't notice.*)
LOUISA: And where is the evidence for *your* talent? How many buildings are actually standing to your credit?
KRACKLITE: A few.
(*He takes off his trousers.*)

LOUISA: (*Affectionately*) Stourley! Six! . . . and a half . . . I'd say . . . though to hear you talk, the world would think there were fifty or more. One of those six buildings is about to be demolished because it stood so long unfinished, one has been changed out of all recognition because others had to complete what you started . . .

(KRACKLITE *has been barely listening – caught putting his nightshirt over his head – he's bent with a pain in his stomach.*)

. . . and there's our house that's so experimental, unfinished and incomplete that rats wouldn't call it a home . . . and now you're wasting your time putting on an exhibition in memory of another architect who also built practically nothing! (*Finally notices his pain.*) What's the matter?

KRACKLITE: Oh – nothing – indigestion. I must have eaten something that disagreed with me. (*Succeeds in pulling on his nightshirt, self-mockingly*) But it's nothing that a little sympathy couldn't cure.

(*He climbs on to the bed rather than gets into it and he makes to put his arms around* LOUISA *– he begins to undo the buttons on* LOUISA*'s nightdress – she doesn't stop him.*)

LOUISA: (*Pleasurably reacting to his attentions*) What's this, Kracklite? Twice in one day?

(*She puts her arms around him.*)

KRACKLITE: Boullée has less than *three* buildings standing to *his* credit, and look at his reputation.

LOUISA: Will they give *you* an exhibition a hundred and eighty years after *your* death?

KRACKLITE: Death – who's talking about death?

(*They start to make love.*)

LOUISA: (*Musing*) Doesn't everyone talk about death in Rome?

A wider shot of the shadowy illuminated room shows the view out of the window on to the darkened Mausoleum of Augustus, with KRACKLITE and LOUISA on the bed in the foreground. After a moment KRACKLITE lets out a cry of pain.

LOUISA: (*Startled*) What's the matter?

KRACKLITE: My stomach! (*He kneels up under the sheet.*)

LOUISA: (*Sarcastically, thwarted and annoyed at the brevity of his love-making*) Thank you! Don't damn well start what you can't finish! (*After a moan from* KRACKLITE) Serves you right, Kracklite! You eat too much! . . . You're always stuffing yourself!

KRACKLITE rolls off her. He is still in pain. LOUISA sits up, now really exasperated. She's too angry to notice his condition . . . She diverts her irritation.

LOUISA: And look at the state of this room! (*Indicates his clothes thrown all over the place*) And we've only been here eight hours . . .

KRACKLITE: (*Even in pain – attempting humour*) That long!?

The pain lessens. LOUISA turns her back on him and covers her head with the sheet. KRACKLITE breathes deeply, holding his stomach. He half-heartedly looks to resume his attentions to LOUISA, but doesn't pursue it. As the pain eases, KRACKLITE relaxes back on the pillows. After a pause, KRACKLITE stretches out and picks up a pen and paper from his bedside table.

LOUISA: (*From under the sheet*) What are you doing now?

KRACKLITE: Oh . . . (*Airily*) pretending I'm twenty-four, wearing a medallion and a double-breasted suit . . . I'm just going to rush off a few new masterpieces . . .

LOUISA: (*Turns and looks at him*) Idiot!

(*She turns away, pulling most of the sheet with her and off him. He doesn't attempt to reclaim it.*)

KRACKLITE sits up in bed drawing. The wind at the open window blows the curtains – the Augustan Mausoleum is dimly seen against the night sky. With the introduction of a contemplative piece of music – henceforth called 'The Melancholy of an Architect' music – he draws quickly and adroitly. After a moment or two – we see what he's been drawing – a series of domed buildings – each dome greater and larger than the one before – the Pantheon . . . the cake-model. The domes have human anatomical connotations . . . references to the human stomach. As we watch, KRACKLITE idly draws whirling intestines that spill from the belly-shaped dome of the last in the series.

KRACKLITE looks up from his drawing. LOUISA is fast asleep beside him. Taking the pillowcase off his pillow, KRACKLITE drapes his bedside lamp, cutting back the light even further. He then throws back the sheet – which tosses his many drawings on to the floor. Holding his stomach, he crosses to the bathroom – turns on the bathroom light – which adds another soft and muted light source to the bedroom. Unseen, KRACKLITE in the bathroom turns on a bathroom tap. LOUISA stirs.

Inside the bathroom, KRACKLITE fills a glass under the cold-water tap and – after the slightest hesitation – thinking that the Rome tap water is unsafe to drink – he drinks. He examines his face in the bathroom mirror. He makes faces. Then, switching the bathroom light on and off, he watches his reflection change shape in the alternate light and gloom.

In the bedroom – LOUISA stirs again. The light in the bathroom – going on and off – flickers alternate gloom and darkness across the bedroom. LOUISA wakes and sits up – she looks towards the bathroom door.

LOUISA: (*Exasperated*) Kracklite! What the hell are you doing?

KRACKLITE does not reply but leaves the light off. There is silence – broken only by the gentle breeze moving the curtains at the window.

LOUISA: (*Drowsily*) Come back to bed.

(*She turns over and lies still.*)

KRACKLITE quietly closes the bathroom door. From the outside we hear the sound of painful retching, and then the sounds of running water and the flushing of the cistern. Quietly the bathroom door opens, the bathroom light is switched off and KRACKLITE, wiping his face with a towel, comes out and walks to the window. To the gradual forefronting of the 'Melancholy of an Architect' music which grows stronger and more insistent – he looks out of the window at the Augustan Mausoleum. On the grassy bank of the first level, he sees two white-clad figures – a man and a woman. They are explicitly making love. KRACKLITE stares hard at them – they look rather like LOUISA and CASPASIAN. KRACKLITE looks towards the bed to reassure himself that LOUISA is there. He goes up to her. She is sleeping soundly. He stands watching her breathing deeply. KRACKLITE puts on his red silk dressing-gown and leaves the bedroom, walking quietly along the moon-lit corridor. He comes out on to the moon-lit deserted piazza and stands looking at the Mausoleum. The lovers have gone. The slight breeze pulls at his dressing-gown and ruffles his hair. He walks around the Mausoleum, looking at it from several viewpoints. It is gaunt and mysterious and intimidating in the moonlight and in its own shadowy floodlighting. It reeks of age, history and death. He stares at it, absent-mindedly stroking his belly – his back against a mammoth Latin inscription on the wall of the Altar of Augustan Peace.

Section Five: Noon, Wednesday, 29 May 1985

SCENE 8: VITTORIANO COLONNADE

Over a wide view of the brightly sunlit Victor Emanuel Building taken from the Piazza de Venezia IO speaks. His authoritative commentary sounds like a continuation of the appreciation of architecture that he was making after the meal at the Pantheon restaurant.

IO: (*Voice over*) . . . the Romans are very equivocal about *this* building. They call it the typewriter or the wedding cake . . . But whatever you think of it – it gives you the most amazing views of Rome. It's like a box at the theatre at which Rome is the play.

On the north terrace – Veronese-style – a banquet is being prepared – tables, side tables, chairs, shining cutlery, glasses, china. Various sombre-suited Italian officials – curators, businessmen – are standing talking. Over by the Forum side of the terrace, KRACKLITE – conspicuous in a white suit – is talking to IO, and looking with great interest and enthusiasm at the views and the building. IO continues.

IO: From here you can see the Colosseum . . . and over here . . .

(IO *takes* KRACKLITE *by the arm and walks him into the centre of the terrace among the busy waiters.*)

. . . you can see Michelangelo's Dome of St Peter's . . . and you can just see Borromimi's Church of St Agnes in the Piazza Navona.

KRACKLITE: . . . and the Tomb of Augustus?
(A group of dark-suited Italian bankers, officials and curators has quietly approached. One of them speaks.)
CASPETTI: . . . difficult to see from here, Signor Kracklite – but undoubtedly there.
IO: (*Turning round*) Ah! . . . Signor Kracklite – let me introduce you. This is Antonio Caspetti, banker with the Scudo d'Oro. Signor Caspetti is our most important benefactor.
(*They shake hands.*)
There is no way that we could manage this exhibition without him.
CASPETTI: And after its undoubted success I hope we can consider a return exhibition in Chicago – perhaps on the Italian architect Piranesi?
IO: Signor Caspetti is a great authority on Piranesi.

While this conversation has been going on, CASPASIAN and LOUISA, who have been talking, leave the colonnade together, followed by a dark-suited Roman official, SALVATORE BATTISTINO.

Section Six: Just after Noon, Wednesday, 29 May 1985

SCENE 9: VITTORIANO MAIN HALL

CASPASIAN and LOUISA have entered the large main hall of the Vittoriano where a buffet has been prepared. Towards one end is a table laid out with flowers and wine glasses. Two waiters behind the table are pouring wine for the guests. Near at hand are small chairs and a wide sofa.

LOUISA and CASPASIAN take glasses of wine offered by a waiter and they sit down on a deeply-sprung, upholstered sofa.

SALVATORE BATTISTINO, the Secretary of the Society – an elderly man, dwarfish and emaciated-looking and in his late seventies – sits down on LOUISA's left-hand side. The other guests – talking and laughing – begin to move down the hall to the refreshment tables.

CASPASIAN: (*Graciously and ironically*) Does Signor Kracklite always travel accompanied by his wife?

LOUISA: (*Smiling*) If it's somewhere interesting – I make sure his ego (*With a forthright and disarming smile at* CASPASIAN, *testing her ability to provoke*) stimulates his physical energy which means I might get pregnant. Boullée *could* be useful. (*She laughs.*)

The ever-predatory CASPASIAN is a little taken aback by such forthrightness. Meanwhile, on her left side, despite his age, BATTISTINO has unashamedly put his hand on LOUISA's leg – above the knee. LOUISA for the moment is so surprised, she pretends not to notice. There is subdued chatter all around. With the minimum of fuss, LOUISA pushes the man's hand away. LOUISA is, on either side, accompanied by handsome youth and senile old age – both predatory.

SCENE 10: VITTORIANO BALCONY

Behind the group on the sofa, KRACKLITE, with IO and the other officials, climbs a short flight of stairs to a dais or platform that overlooks the scene. Behind them is a large, wooden-framed window on to the sky. The four men hold wine glasses.

CASPETTI: I remember, Signor Kracklite, coming across a drawing by Boullée when I was ten years old – it reminded me, I must admit, of Hell . . . no doubt it was a childish idea . . . but it hasn't entirely left me. I hope that your exhibition will change my first impressions . . . ?

KRACKLITE: (*With a smile*) I must confess his designs have always reminded me of Heaven.

IO: Heaven or Hell, I suspect, took longer to create than nine months, which is, unfortunately, all we have . . .

PASTARRI: A period long enough to have produced Boullée!

(*Laughter.*)

JULIO: Which means – if we intend to open on his birthday – that he must have been conceived about now.

(*Laughter.*)

TRETTORIO: Then his mother is to be congratulated on her timing.

(*Laughter.*)

IO: (*To* KRACKLITE) Doctor Gallo Trettorio, expert on the Medicine of the Classical World.

The crowd of officials are like black crows around an over-dressed, over-colourful interloper. They are courteous and polite – but distant. KRACKLITE looks curiously at TRETTORIO and shakes his hand; they stare at one another for a few moments.

SCENE 11: VITTORIANO MAIN HALL

On the sofa, the conversation continues.

CASPASIAN: Kracklite must know that Boullée is not *that* well known in Italy.

LOUISA: (*Laughing*) Boullée is not *that* well known anywhere. In Texas (*With a laugh*) Kracklite was accused of inventing him.

CASPASIAN: Maybe he is an ideal architect for your husband to invent. However . . . thanks to Kracklite, we have nearly a million dollars to persuade the Italian public that Boullée is not a fiction.

LOUISA: It's a lot of money.

CASPASIAN: It's expensive to put on a large art exhibition in Rome.

LOUISA: (*With a sly smile*) . . . and you are in charge of the purse strings . . . ?

CASPASIAN: (*With a smile back*) Not entirely . . . but almost.

LOUISA: (*Provocatively*) You are very young to be entrusted with so much money.

CASPASIAN: (*With return provocation*) . . . and you are very young to be entrusted with such an elderly husband . . . ? (*They both laugh.*)

LOUISA's laughter is cut short by a second attempt by BATTISTINO to run his hand up her leg. She doesn't know quite how to react – he looks an elderly and dignified gentleman. She moves and brushes his hand away – and tries to stare him out. He doesn't return her stare.

SCENE 12: VITTORIANO BALCONY

Up on the dais or platform, KRACKLITE is leaning against the large fan-shaped window so that it just takes his weight – he notices that it gives slightly in its frame – he experimentally tests its giving power – and watches a split in the woodwork slightly open and close where the frame meets the stonework. IO notices what KRACKLITE is doing. KRACKLITE does it with an architect's curiosity.

CASPETTI: Stourley – be careful! Zucconi, the architect of this building, spent all the money on the marble. He didn't like wood and he skimped on the carpentry.

PASTARRI: (*Sardonically*) He hated Joseph. He loved the Virgin Mary. You see – he didn't believe in the Virgin Birth. Joseph was forty and the Virgin Mary was fourteen – (*With a smile*) that's about the same age difference as you and your wife, isn't it, Signor Kracklite?

KRACKLITE: (*With a smile*) Approximately. (*Changes the subject.*) But I thought *all* Catholics believed in the Virgin Birth.

JULIO: Not outside of marriage.

(*Laughter.*)

CASPETTI: Do *you* believe in the Virgin Birth, Signor Kracklite?

KRACKLITE: (*With a sudden seriousness*) At the moment, Signor Caspetti, I'll settle for *any* sort of birth.

JULIO: (*A serious inquiry*) You have no children?

KRACKLITE: (*With flippancy masking embarrassment*) Not to my knowledge.

(*Laughter.*)

SCENE 13: VITTORIANO MAIN HALL

Down on the gallery floor, CASPASIAN and LOUISA are still talking – BATTISTINO quietly eyeing LOUISA and admiring her legs. LOUISA tries to smile at BATTISTINO to break the uncomfortableness he is causing her – but he refuses to catch her eye.

LOUISA: Stourley *once* believed that art – in his case building great buildings – would buy him immortality . . .

CASPASIAN: Doesn't he believe it any more?

LOUISA: Now he only half believes it. However . . . he has an insurance policy which *I* am supposed to supply . . . if he fails with his architecture he realizes that his immortality is probably best achieved through a son.

CASPASIAN: (*With an ironic smile*) It seems to me, Signora Kracklite, that you have serious doubts about both his ambitions.

LOUISA: (*With a wry smile*) I have had several miscarriages, Signor Speckler – almost the same number as Kracklite has of unsatisfactory buildings . . . which means that both of us are still in the planning stage . . . ? Whereas Kracklite gets disillusioned with his projects, I get anxious – both of us could be accused of premature delivery.

SALVATORE's hand has begun to travel up LOUISA's leg. When it has reached her thigh under her dress – LOUISA gets up brusquely – the elderly man who has been leaning his weight against her, topples sideways – the space suddenly vacated. He lays there gasping for breath like a fish out of water. For a moment everyone watches him and then they gather around, loosening his collar, opening his jacket. He dribbles and his body jerks. People none too discreetly hold their noses. From afar KRACKLITE watches fascinated. CASPASIAN has put his arm around LOUISA – which does not go unnoticed by KRACKLITE. As from nowhere, photographers rush in to take pictures. A little to one side, FLAVIA appears – she too takes photographs – perhaps a little more discreetly than the others. She concentrates more on LOUISA – and eventually KRACKLITE – rather than on BATTISTINO. She winks at CASPASIAN, who returns her confidence. She gives him a brown envelope.

LOUISA: (*Shocked – her confidence temporarily upset*) Did you see what he was doing!

CASPASIAN: (*Amused*) He always had a certain reputation.

KRACKLITE, with IO, is coming in their direction to see what all the fuss is about.

CASPASIAN: (*With a sly smile – steering her away – but not preventing the photographers from taking pictures of* LOUISA *and himself together*) But you see what has happened. Now Kracklite is honoured by Roman publicity.
(*He indicates* KRACKLITE *and speaks with amused sarcasm – the photographers turn their attention to* KRACKLITE.)
Now perhaps (*Waving his hand around at the excited crowd*) – who knows – your husband and his – (*Corrects himself with a*

smile) our – exhibition have been given a small head start . . . (*With a smile*) and it is you who has provided it for him – but I suspect, Signora Kracklite, that has always been the case. (*They exchange significant looks.*)

KRACKLITE, arriving near the couch, watches the sick man with curiosity. SALVATORE's collar and tie have been undone, his shoelaces untied and his trouser belt loosened. The photographers snap KRACKLITE and the comatose BATTISTINO in the same frame. So does FLAVIA.

Section Seven: Lunchtime, Wednesday, 29 May 1985

SCENE 14: VITTORIANO LUNCH

On the high colonnade overlooking Rome and the Piazza de Venezia, the guests are assembled for lunch.

KRACKLITE: You Italians do a great deal of eating.

MORI: It's a social habit started when things got bad under Augustus . . .

TRETTORIO: . . . and things have been bad ever since.

PASTARRI: Augustus' wife Livia was an anorexic – couldn't stand her husband making a pig of himself . . . but he had the constitution of an ox, he'd consume anything.

(KRACKLITE *notices that* LOUISA *is not touching the figs* –CASPASIAN *is continually passing the figs to* KRACKLITE *who looks at them and then at* CASPASIAN *and* LOUISA – *they are laughing – but apparently not at him.*)

. . . just like contemporary architects?

(KRACKLITE *gives him a hard look.*)

MORI: Are you a modern architect, Mr Kracklite?

KRACKLITE: No more modern than I should be . . .

MARCOLONNA: No more modern than Boullée, would you say?

FLAVIA: (*Who has been listening with amusement*) Replicas of whose buildings now appear regularly in every Totalitarian Capital in the world? Peking, Moscow, East Berlin . . .?

KRACKLITE: (*With a smile*) . . . and Rome, Signorina Speckler?

FLAVIA: Boullée didn't design buildings, Signor Kracklite – he just designed monuments.

KRACKLITE: (*With a smile*) Are you saying that Boullée was the first Fascist architect?

FLAVIA: (*Wryly*) Ask my brother.

CASPASIAN: (*Ignoring his sister and with returned provocation to* KRACKLITE) Do you think that Mussolini admired Boullée?

FLAVIA: (*Quick as a flash and with some spite*) Albert Speer did! . . . and Speer was Hitler's architect.

FLAVIA and CASPASIAN exchange antagonistic smiles – suggesting years of sibling rivalry . . . and much more. KRACKLITE is surprised by FLAVIA's vehemence – he looks expectantly at LOUISA whose face is deliberately blank – neither agreeing or disputing FLAVIA's insinuation, but enjoying the accusations that are aimed at KRACKLITE's hero.

TRETTORIO: Augustus certainly would have. Just look at his tomb.

LOUISA: (*With a smile*) I can't help it – it's outside our bedroom window.

TRETTORIO: (*Nonchalantly*) Well, his wife chose it – after she'd made sure he would fit inside it after all the trouble she'd taken.

KRACKLITE: Trouble?

CASPASIAN: Augustus felt this dryness at the back of his throat . . . and then a cold shiver across his shoulders . . .
(*He begins to play-act – mainly for* LOUISA*'s benefit – she is amused.*)
. . . a desire to urinate, a pain like a poker in the small of the back . . . a desire to vomit . . . it was obviously poison . . .

LOUISA: (*With a smile*) Are you sure you studied architecture and not medicine?

CASPASIAN: . . . then his neck became stiff . . . his gums began to ache . . . his ears to sing . . . his eyes to flutter . . .

MORI: God! – a very stagey death.

PASTARRI: Are *you* building a tomb for *your* husband, Senora Kracklite? (*There is laughter.*)

CASPASIAN: . . . the buttons popped off his jacket . . .

LOUISA: Jacket? Are you sure?

CASPASIAN: . . . his feet slipped as though on ice . . . a gallon of yellow bile erupted from his mouth . . . his eyes . . .

FLAVIA: Caspasian! (*Brusquely*) That's enough! I'm eating.

CASPASIAN: Sorry, Flavia.

(*He's being a little sarcastic – but there is evidence that his sister normally overrules him.*)

It's just a history lesson . . . (*Stage-whispers*) for foreigners.

KRACKLITE – feeling uncomfortable through CASPASIAN's theatrical anecdote – gets up and exits with as much dignity as can be managed – he leaves without saying a word. The other guests naturally wonder where he has gone and comment about his hurried exit. LOUISA looks concerned and wonders whether she should go after him.

SCENE 15: VITTORIANO TOILET

After the wide spaces of the Piazza de Venezia, the claustrophobic space of the atrium lavatory in the Victor Emanuel building. KRACKLITE is leaning over the single sink – he has just vomited his lunch into the basin. The taps are running. He stands – his eyes closed – recovering. He straightens up and leans against the wall. He takes out a large handkerchief and wipes his forehead. He then washes his hands, stares at himself in the stained mirror above the basin. His reverie is broken by the sound of a flushing WC behind him. He straightens his tie and, still wiping his mouth on his handkerchief, is surprised to see BATTISTINO – looking fit and well – emerge from the row of cubicles.

He is carrying his shoes and his tie. BATTISTINO nods at KRACKLITE and, standing before the mirror, begins to tie his tie.

KRACKLITE: (*Nonplussed*) Are you all right?

(BATTISTINO *speaks no English and smiles back.* CASPASIAN *enters from the inner staircase.*)

CASPASIAN: Of course he's all right. (*In Italian*) Salvatore, Signor Kracklite asks if you are feeling all right.

BATTISTINO: (*With a smile to* KRACKLITE *– and in Italian*) Of course, Signor Kracklite. Thank you.

(BATTISTINO *sits down on a wooden bench to put on his shoes.*)

KRACKLITE: (*Still surprised*) But he was at death's door just now!

(CASPASIAN *sits with* BATTISTINO *on the bench and takes on the brown envelope that we saw* FLAVIA *give him earlier.*)

CASPASIAN: An exhibition like this – in Rome – about an obscure French architect and organized by an . . . (*About to say 'obscure' – but bites his tongue*) . . . American architect – needs all the publicity it can get . . . wouldn't you say?

(*He winks exaggeratedly at* KRACKLITE.)

He gives BATTISTINO half the banknotes he takes out of the brown envelope. He keeps the rest for himself. Nonplussed and still wiping his mouth and his forehead, KRACKLITE leaves the lavatory. BATTISTINO and CASPASIAN exchange a smile while BATTISTINO ties his shoelaces.

SCENE 16: VITTORIANO ATRIUM

On the first landing above the atrium, there is a desk area for the welcoming of visitors and Press to the inauguration of the Exhibition. Laid out on a counter are art-books and postcards. Several guests are grouped together talking. KRACKLITE, still wiping his face with his handkerchief, approaches his wife, who is talking with FLAVIA at the entrance desk. So as not to be overheard, KRACKLITE speaks in a half-whisper to his wife as he hands his cloakroom tag to a woman behind the desk who finds his briefcase.

KRACKLITE: I'm going back to the hotel . . . to work.

LOUISA: But we've only just met them – you can't rush off.

KRACKLITE: (*Unconvincingly*) I want to get started.

LOUISA: (*In his best interests*) Stourley, *this* is where you should start. These are the people that are going to make it happen.

KRACKLITE: No, I must go. I don't feel so good. Why don't you go sight-seeing! The Specklers will take you.

LOUISA: God! (*Exasperated*) Stourley – why don't *you* take me? Let's walk for a few hours . . . we could have a leisurely meal . . . (*With a touch of coquetry – touching his belly and thigh under the cover of his coat.*) and an early night.

KRACKLITE: (*Holding her away*) Look, Louisa – you go with the Specklers and I'll see you this evening at the concert . . . Say goodbye for me.

LOUISA: (*Sadly and angrily under her breath*) Anything for Boullée!

All the time he has been speaking to LOUISA, KRACKLITE has noticed – in the postcard racks – a postcard of a statue of Augustus and postcards of the Augusteum. He picks out a portrait of Augustus and looks at it closely. The Augustus statue is in the heroic mould and is nearly naked. Its stomach area is clearly delineated.
KRACKLITE deliberates and then swiftly takes a handful of the postcards – both of the Augusteum and Augustus and hides them in his jacket pocket. As he leaves he sees that FLAVIA has seen him steal the cards.
LOUISA watches KRACKLITE go. FLAVIA comes forward and, linking arms with LOUISA, leads her off.
KRACKLITE walks across the atrium to huge double doors on the other side.

Section Eight: After Lunch, Wednesday, 29 May 1985

SCENE 17: VITTORIANO PHOTOCOPIER
KRACKLITE enters a large dark room full of looming plaster statuary. (Later the room is converted into Kracklite's workroom.) A section of the room glows with the mysterious green light of a large photocopying machine. KRACKLITE takes out one of the Augustus postcards and lifting the photocopier lid – it throws an eerie green glow on his face – he arranges the postcard on the photographic bed.
He selects a button and the machine starts – adding orange and white lights to the green. Twelve large, enlarged photocopied stomachs of Augustus roll out of the machine's mouth; with painful, mechanical noises – halfway between coughing, choking and screaming – the machine 'gives birth' to twelve stomachs. When the machine stops, KRACKLITE picks up an enlargement and examines it. The enlargements are damp and a little shiny. He lifts his shirt and feels for his stomach. He takes an enlarged photograph of the Augustus 'belly' from the machine and looks down at his own belly. He identifies his stomach with the stomach of Augustus and feels the pain as though it's Augustus who is suffering.

Section Nine: Evening, Wednesday, 29 May 1985

SCENE 18: FORO ITALICO

It's getting dark and raining. LOUISA and KRACKLITE are on their way to a concert. They have the use of a large black car which is parked on the edge of the Foro Italico. LOUISA is sitting – somewhat impatiently – in the car, listening to an Italian Linguaphone tape. The rain is dribbling down the window. KRACKLITE – a distant figure – is taking photographs of the statues around the open stadium.

Several statues are seen momentarily illuminated by KRACKLITE's flash. A yellow sunset dramatizes the grey sky. The statues are aggressive and, in the context, surreal. KRACKLITE looks at them, curious about their exuberant health, their bogus, assertive vitality. It contrasts with his own. He sits and stares, takes a clutch of postcards from his inside jacket pocket. He is wearing a raincoat over a dinner suit. He takes out a screw-top pen and writes on the back of a postcard of the Mausoleum of Augustus.

First the date – *29 May 1985* – and then,

> *Monsieur Boullée,*
> *I hope you don't mind me writing to you like this, I feel I know you well enough to talk to you. I think my wife is poisoning me.*

LOUISA, in the car, beeps the horn . . . KRACKLITE pauses and looks towards the car – but then resumes writing.

> *I think it's part of her general animosity towards you . . . you can laugh . . . but I'm serious.*
>
> *Yours, with respect,*
> *Stourley Kracklite*

As an afterthought, he writes *Architect* after his signature.

The postcard is already addressed in his handwriting. LOUISA beeps the car horn again. Reluctantly KRACKLITE gets up. He walks slowly back to the car. He passes a postbox on the way and posts the letter. He gets into the car – into the driving seat.

LOUISA: (*Impatiently*) Come on – we are going to be late!
(*She looks at him – he looks ill.*)
Are you feeling all right? You look green.

KRACKLITE switches the engine on and the dashboard lights reflect viridian-green light up on to his face. He puts his face into a position to catch the dashboard lights. He grins sarcastically at her.

KRACKLITE: Is that better?

SCENE 19: THE CONCERT

A concert of modern music – the music of the film being played in concert-platform conditions – is attended by an invited audience in formal dress.

Occupying a row – in the same sequence of seats that they occupied in front of the Pantheon – KRACKLITE, LOUISA, CASPASIAN, IO and FLAVIA are all listening to the music.

KRACKLITE – in evening suit – looks ill – and fidgets. Eventually he whispers in LOUISA's ear.

KRACKLITE: I'm just going to get a drink of water – it's hot in here.

LOUISA: Are you all right? Shall I come with you?

He shakes his head and, trying to create a minimum of disturbance, gets up to leave. FLAVIA makes way for him.

LOUISA and FLAVIA both watch him leave the hall. They look at one another and then return their attention to the concert platform.

He virtually runs into the cloakroom and vomits into a sink. The cloakroom is palatial – well appointed with marble floors, gold taps, high ceilings and an echoic resonance. He runs the taps full on and douses his face – then swabs it with paper towels. He looks into the mirror and examines his tongue. He unfolds a photocopy of Augustus taken from his pocket, and, looking at his watch, marks Augustus' belly with the conditions of his symptoms. All this time – there has been the sound of a violin being played very close at hand. The music now stops and a man comes out of a toilet cubicle – he's holding a violin under his chin, a bow in his teeth and he's pulling up his trousers. On the floor is a shabby red violin case. We've seen it somewhere before, on the station platform at Ventimiglia. He nods at KRACKLITE and gives him a searching look. KRACKLITE puts his Augustan photocopy away in his inside jacket pocket.

VIOLINIST: (*In Italian*) Are you the conductor?

KRACKLITE: Pardon?

VIOLINIST: (*In English*) Are you the conductor?

KRACKLITE: I'm afraid not. Do you normally practise in there?

VIOLINIST: Oh yes – the acoustics are good and the bowels are rested. It's a compensation for being too late to join the orchestra . . . Nerves go to my stomach . . . the trouble is . . . (*Gives* KRACKLITE *a searching look.*) Are you all right?

KRACKLITE: Yes, thank you.

VIOLINIST: The trouble is – the space is a little cramped . . . (*Indicates his elbows*) Elbows . . .

KRACKLITE: Pardon?

VIOLINIST: Restricted bowing.

The VIOLINIST returns to the cubicle – sits on the seat and begins to play – with sweeps of rhythmic exuberance – he occasionally bumps his elbows on the walls – indicating the problem with a nod of his head. KRACKLITE leans on a basin and listens. Behind him the door opens and FLAVIA looks in. The open door lets in distant music from the concert hall.

FLAVIA: Are you all right, Stourley?

KRACKLITE: Yes, thanks – I'm not so keen on symphonic music – (*Significantly*) too much collaboration. I like a solo instrument.

(*He indicates the* VIOLINIST *with a smile.*)

FLAVIA: May I take a photograph?

KRACKLITE: Ask him.

(*He indicates the* VIOLINIST.)

FLAVIA smiles and the VIOLINIST smiles back. She takes a flashlight photograph of the VIOLINIST who exuberantly plays for her in the toilet cubicle with KRACKLITE watching. She speaks to KRACKLITE while she takes another.

FLAVIA: You ought to see a doctor.

KRACKLITE: (*With a smile*) Who? (*Indicating the* VIOLINIST) Him or me?

Section Ten: Night of 29–30 May 1985

SCENE 20: APARTMENT WITH FIGS

At night in the Kracklite hotel bedroom. Prominently placed beside Kracklite's side of the bed is a plate of figs. His side of the bed is also littered with books and papers. KRACKLITE is writing and drawing on a piece of foolscap – it's apparent that he is drawing figs. LOUISA is asleep.

KRACKLITE: Louisa . . . do you like figs?

LOUISA: (*Half asleep*) Yes.

KRACKLITE: Then why do you persistently avoid them?

LOUISA: Do I?

KRACKLITE: (*Turning and picking up the plate of figs from his bedside table – they are already peeled and cut – the knife is still on the plate*) Louisa – I want you to eat these figs. (*He hovers over her with the plate of figs.*)

LOUISA: (*Still not fully awake*) Kracklite – for God's sake – not now.

KRACKLITE: Why not now, for God's sake?

LOUISA: (*Falling back into a deep sleep*) It's one o'clock and I'm tired.

KRACKLITE: Just take them with a glass of wine.

(*He makes to take the glass of wine from his bedside table.*)

LOUISA: (*A little more roused*) Are you mad, Kracklite?

KRACKLITE: (*Exploding*) Damn well eat them!

KRACKLITE takes a peeled fig from the plate and tries to ram it in her mouth. For a moment they struggle – the fig juice staining the sheets. The fig gets lost in the sheets and KRACKLITE grabs another from the plate and tries to ram that in her mouth. LOUISA's first reaction was surprise, then anger – now she is afraid. She struggles out of the bed and kneels on the floor trying to get away from him.

LOUISA: Stourley – what the hell's got into you? Christ – are you mad?

Free of the sheet, LOUISA backs away to the bedroom wall – for a moment it looks as though KRACKLITE will follow her there – then realizing the stupidity of it, he pauses and then sinks back into the bed – a rich, ripe, peeled fig in his fingers – with the juice running down his wrist on to his arm. He watches the juice run.

KRACKLITE: I see.

LOUISA: You see what?

KRACKLITE: You say you like figs – but you never touch them.

LOUISA: You're rambling.

KRACKLITE: I want to see what happens to you when you eat figs – that's all.

There is a long pause while LOUISA digests this information. KRACKLITE takes a tissue from a box by the bed and wipes the fig juice off his arm.

KRACKLITE: Don't stand there – you'll catch cold – get back into bed.

LOUISA: (*Conciliatory*) Figs are supposed to be an aphrodisiac . . . aren't they? (*Humouring him*) Is that why you want me to eat them?

KRACKLITE: Forget it!

LOUISA: No – I won't damn well forget it – you come on like a madman and then say forget it – What the hell's the matter with you?

KRACKLITE gets out of bed. He picks up the plate of figs. He goes to the window. Warily, LOUISA crosses the room and goes into the bathroom – she stands by the door.

KRACKLITE: I wanted to see if you're as frightened of eating figs as I am.

LOUISA: Frightened? Do you think I ought to be frightened? Stourley? (*Genuinely worried*) Don't you think you ought to see a doctor?

KRACKLITE takes a mock-threatening step in her direction and she quickly shuts and locks the bathroom door. KRACKLITE smiles to himself. He looks at his watch – its luminous dial shows up in the dark – it says 1.05 a.m. He switches on the desk lamp over his books and papers near the window. On the desk are the magazines featuring the crude, flashlight photos taken at the Exhibition Inauguration – of KRACKLITE looming over the comatose and apparently sick BATTISTINO and of CASPASIAN with his arms around LOUISA.

KRACKLITE lifts some of the papers on his untidy desk and

uncovers the photocopy enlargements of the Augustan stomachs. He spreads them out – some of them have been marked – the stomach shaded – and each one shows a time. He takes up a pen and marks a new photocopy and adds the new time – *30 MAY 1985 – 1.05 a.m.*

He then takes the plate of figs and, one by one, he hurls them through the window into the street. From outside, the squashed figs land with a messy plop on the road surface.

Looking back at the hotel – KRACKLITE – a large naked figure – can be seen standing at the lit window hurling the figs out into the night. One of the figs lands with a splat in front of the camera.

Section Eleven: Evening, Thursday, 6 June 1985

SCENE 21: DOCTOR'S CONSULTING ROOM

KRACKLITE comes up in a gloomy lift – his head illuminated from above, throwing his eyes deep in shadow. He looks straight ahead of him. He steps out into a corridor. He knocks on a door. The doctor's room is shadowy, full of books, Roman statuary, obelisks, prints, paintings. It looks as though the doctor is more of an antiquary or an archaeologist than a doctor of medicine.

DOCTOR: Good evening. Sit down. Put your hands on the table.

KRACKLITE does as he's told – submissively. The DOCTOR looks at papers on his desk. KRACKLITE's hands stray back to his head.

DOCTOR: Are you an architect?

KRACKLITE: Yes.

DOCTOR: Why?

KRACKLITE: (*The question phases him – he pauses before answering*) Why are you a doctor?

DOCTOR: To rebuild bodies? (*Shrugs*) Is that good enough?

KRACKLITE: You start at a disadvantage then?

DOCTOR: How's that?

KRACKLITE: You can only *re*build – you could never build a body from scratch.

DOCTOR: In Rome it's impossible to build a *building* from scratch.

KRACKLITE: I'm not from Rome.
(*There is a pause as the two men eye one another.*)
DOCTOR: (*Playfully*) Would you say that there was an illness peculiar to architects?
KRACKLITE: (*Without hesitation*) Melancholia?
(*They both smile.*)
DOCTOR: Put your hands on the table and turn the palms over.
(KRACKLITE *does so.*)
Why were you holding your head when your trouble is in your stomach?
KRACKLITE: How did you know that?
DOCTOR: The backs of your hands.
(KRACKLITE *looks at the backs of his hands.*)
What do you think is wrong with you?
KRACKLITE: If I was back home in the States, I could probably believe it was gallstones.
DOCTOR: And in Rome?
KRACKLITE: Well . . . I'm told Augustus suffered from indigestion.
DOCTOR: (*Mildly surprised*) Often.
KRACKLITE: Often?
DOCTOR: (*Smiling*) He was the victim of poison seventeen times at least.
KRACKLITE: (*Quickly*) Who poisoned him? His wife?
DOCTOR: (*Looking curiously at* KRACKLITE) If you were being poisoned – you'd know it. What are your symptoms?
KRACKLITE: I've made a note.
(*He pulls the photos of the Augustan stomach from his inside jacket pocket.*)
DOCTOR: (*Curiously looking at the photos and at* KRACKLITE) The stomach of Augustus.
KRACKLITE: You know it?
DOCTOR: There are seventeen statues of Augustus in Rome . . .
KRACKLITE: (*With a wry smile*) One for each set of poisoned figs?
DOCTOR: (*Looking at the photo*) Do you have such an heroic abdomen? Take off your shirt.
(KRACKLITE *takes off his shirt.*)

Where does it ache?
KRACKLITE: (*Indicating*) Here.
(*The* DOCTOR *touches him and* KRACKLITE *winces.*)
DOCTOR: Where did you eat your figs?
KRACKLITE: It started in a restaurant near the Pantheon.
DOCTOR: A fine building. You are married?
KRACKLITE: Yes.
DOCTOR: She is Italian?
KRACKLITE: Her parents were Italian – yes – (*With a significant look*) from Umbria.
DOCTOR: It's a fine fig-growing area. Do you sleep well at night?
KRACKLITE: (*Perplexed*) I did – before I came to Rome.
(*The* DOCTOR *silently examines* KRACKLITE *– prodding his stomach.*)
DOCTOR: Mr Architect – let me assure you – you are not being poisoned. I suggest that you are suffering from dyspepsia, fatigue, over-excitement, excess – and unfamiliar food, lack of exercise and too much coffee – maybe also too much egotism. Your Augustan stomachs are nevertheless amusing. Take these – obey the instructions. (*Gives him a phial of plain-looking pills, then picks up the photos again.*) Augustus wasn't, by all accounts, a fat man – (*Provocatively*) at least not as fat as you – and just consider what *he* did.
(*He hands back the photo.*)
KRACKLITE: Is Augustus a hero of yours?
DOCTOR: Not particularly – he amuses me.
KRACKLITE: You are always being amused.
DOCTOR: What frame of mind better suits a doctor?
KRACKLITE: And what amuses you about Augustus?
DOCTOR: For a start – his tomb.
KRACKLITE: His tomb?
(*There is a large Piranesi engraving of the Mausoleum of Augustus hanging on the wall.*)
DOCTOR: The Augusteum has been a fortress, a vineyard, a garden, a bull-ring, a concert hall, a display ground for fireworks, a dance hall and an air-raid shelter, an arsenal, a prison, a brothel, a barn, a chapel, a stable, a cinema . . . and, of course, a car-park

and a public urinal and Mussolini planned to be buried there . . . it's now full of cats and tramps . . . mostly American vagrants . . . could you hope your tomb would be so versatile? (*Looks at his watch.*) When you send me a cheque, enclose an extra one hundred dollar note for services to Architecture . . . (*Looks up*) will you? Now get dressed and come to the window. It's nearly seven o'clock – the sun will pass over the Colosseum in a few minutes. You ought to watch it.

The DOCTOR walks over to the door of the surgery, opens it on to a large sitting room with french windows which he throws open. There is a shallow balcony overlooking the Colosseum lit by the sunset – a splendid, breath-taking view. KRACKLITE follows – putting on his shirt and buttoning it over his belly that glows orange in the setting sun. They both look out directly into the low sunlight. They see – as do we – the Colosseum and the Arch of Constantine beyond.

Time-lapse 3

As we watch, the real-time sunset is slowly, gradually, speeded up into exaggerated time. The sun goes down, the floodlights come on, night falls, the traffic continues to streak the darkness, the moon rises. The shot lasts some 30 seconds – accompanied by the sonorous 'barbarous' music we have associated with the time-lapse sequences of Rome before.

Section Twelve: Noon, Wednesday, 31 July 1985

SCENE 22: PIAZZA DEL POPOLO

On a very warm noon, KRACKLITE is at the Piazza del Popolo. He is looking down towards the Corso – he is either sitting on the edge of the fountain in the centre of the Piazza or sitting in a car – with the roof open. Either way, we can hear the Linguaphone tapes on the car cassette – with a more advanced vocabulary than last time. He is sweating and a little breathless. He occasionally bends double and bites his lower lip – to ease the ache in his stomach. The pain is not excessive, but none the less intimidating. He is writing a postcard to Boullée. The picture on the postcard is a view of what he can see in front of him – the two churches that frame the Corso. He repeatedly looks at the view.

Wed 31 July '85

Dear Monsieur Boullée,
I now have the suspicion that these Italians want to put the exhibition on all by themselves. Suddenly everyone claims to know all about you . . . they are at last claiming you were God's gift to Architecture . . . one of them said this morning that you were Italian, not French . . . all those years when they couldn't have cared less . . . I bet you're laughing . . .

KRACKLITE: (*Looking up from his writing*) I wish I was laughing.

Section Thirteen: Afternoon, Wednesday, 31 July 1985

SCENE 23: VITTORIANO BASEMENT WORK ROOMS
The exhibition work rooms and offices have been set up in the carvernous basement of the Victor Emanuel Building. KRACKLITE has summoned a meeting. There are trestle tables, side tables and plans, around which are grouped the exhibition organizers. KRACKLITE has taken off his jacket and rolled up his sleeves – he looks efficient and businesslike, but he is irritable and hectoring – the Italians are unperturbed at his haranguing. BATTISTINO is quietly dozing. Prominently placed on the table is a simple gyroscope – a toy KRACKLITE occasionally plays with.

KRACKLITE: The various departments take forever to produce their estimates and the builders are charging too much. It's a month now since the research material from Paris was ordered . . . (*Looks around at the others.*) The insurance guarantors are still worried because they say I want to do too much, in too short a time, with too little money, and according to Caspasian's figures we've spent 400 million lire already with precious little to show for it. We have barely six months to go if we plan to open – as we must! – on Boullée's birthday!

Proceedings are interrupted, to KRACKLITE's annoyance, by two waiters entering with two trolleys laden with cakes and jellies, savouries of some complexity, silver coffee-pots, cognac and brandy. The members around the table stretch and relax. KRACKLITE leans over to IO.

KRACKLITE: Why are they so difficult?

IO: Difficult?

KRACKLITE: Everything has to be debated, and qualified and contradicted . . .

IO: (*Laughing*) They are not difficult – you have them excited. This is the first time that the Victorio Emanuale has been used for an exhibition. You ought to be grateful.

KRACKLITE: Grateful? And where's Caspasian? He's supposed to be here.

JULIO: Caspasian's out buying.

KRACKLITE: Buying what?

IO: (*Smiling*) He's having the staircase repainted. He's ordered two thousand litres of blue matt emulsion and the same of green.

KRACKLITE: Green and blue! There's going to be no green or blue in my exhibition! Boullée hated those colours!

JULIO: Where on earth did you discover that?

FREDERICO enters, pushing a trolley with a model of the Vittoriano – made of card and plaster – the roof of the model has been 'exploded', and the streets around the gallery indicated with model cars. The members gather around – holding their coffee cups.

IO: Caspasian's found twenty-five thousand dollars' worth of laser equipment.

KRACKLITE: What the hell for?

IO: He's got a plan to use laser beams to join all the buildings in Rome that influenced Boullée.

KRACKLITE: (*Irritated*) God, he's going to turn this exhibition into a fairground! He's got no business doing that!

JULIO: Don't you think it's a good idea?

KRACKLITE: (*Turning his irritation on to the model*) What's the scale?

FREDERICO: It's what you asked for.
KRACKLITE: In centimetres or inches?
FREDERICO: Centimetres! No self-respecting architect uses inches.
IO: Did Boullée use inches?
JULIO: (*With a laugh*) He used Boullées.
(*Laughter.*)
How long are they?
FREDERICO: The distance from the nose to the navel. All his buildings are based on human anatomy.
IO: He certainly wasn't a prude!
FREDERICO: (*A barbed question despite the banter*) Are you a prude, Signor Kracklite?
KRACKLITE: (*With a smug smile*) Ask my wife.
FREDERICO: (*Leaning over to* IO *and only half whispering*) Ask your son to ask his wife.

Although most of the members around the table didn't hear the remark – covered in background chatter and the clatter of cups – KRACKLITE did. He lunges out and punches FREDERICO on the nose. FREDERICO recoils – his nose bleeding. There is a surprised hush.

FREDERICO: What the hell was that for?
KRACKLITE: (*Very cool*) To prove – if proof were needed – that you bleed easily – no more and no less.
IO: (*To* KRACKLITE) He deserved it – but it was an unwise show of anger.

Section Fourteen: Morning, Friday, 2 August 1985

SCENE 24: CASPASIAN AND LOUISA IN APARTMENT

In the Kracklite apartment. From the inside, the door opens, letting in LOUISA and CASPASIAN. The room is a mess – papers scattered about, clothes left on the bed – trays of food, coffee cups, etc. Books are piled up in heaps as though pushed there by the shovel of a small bulldozer. Hundreds of coloured postcards of Rome litter the room. The fastidious CASPASIAN almost noticeably wrinkles his nose. He places a load of parcels he has been carrying for LOUISA onto the bed.

LOUISA: God! – he turns everywhere he lives into a pigsty.

CASPASIAN: What does he work with? A bulldozer? (*Moving to the desk by the window*) What's this?

(*He has lifted a file and Kracklite's photocopies of the Augustan stomachs have fallen on to the desk top.*)

LOUISA: What's what? (*Glancing towards the desk as she changes her shoes*) Oh – something for the exhibition.

CASPASIAN: No – look!

(*He spreads the photocopy blow-ups on the desk and takes two more Augustan stomachs from the wastebasket – they are marked and dated with day, month, hour and minute – he holds them up for* LOUISA *to see.*)

What's he doing? Does he think he's Augustus?

LOUISA: No – he thinks he's Boullée.

(*She's changing her shoes – she's dressing for warmer weather and an open-air picnic – and not without calculation she is contriving to show* CASPASIAN *a great deal of leg – he notices.*)

CASPASIAN: Where is Kracklite now?

LOUISA: Oh – I don't know – out marching around Rome somewhere. He's out when I wake up and he's asleep when I come in. I've seen him three times this week, once at the Gallery when he shouted at me, once when he took me to the cinema and fell asleep . . . and I think we spent one breakfast together.

CASPASIAN: (*Looking at the photos with amusement*) What are the markings for?

(*She looks over his shoulder at the photos that are marked in coloured inks.*)

LOUISA: Oh – he's obsessed with his stomach. (*With a smile*) Perhaps he thinks he is going to have a baby.

CASPASIAN: When are *you* going to have a baby?

LOUISA: (*Smiling*) *You* could have waited for me in the lobby.

CASPASIAN: I *could* have done . . . You would look very beautiful pregnant . . . (*After a significant pause*) if I may say so . . . (*Slyly*) you've put on a little weight since you've been in Rome . . . and if you became pregnant . . .? (*He has guessed.*) You would put on a little more . . . just here . . .

(CASPASIAN *touches* LOUISA'*s lower neck cautiously – to see if he should try touching her breasts. She turns away – but not brusquely.*)

LOUISA: *You* seem to know a lot about it.

CASPASIAN: . . . and here.

(*He cautiously touches her backside.*)

LOUISA: Do you take afternoon classes in obstetrics?

CASPASIAN: Architects ought to know about everything – reproduction . . . gender . . . sex . . . expecially sex.

LOUISA: Really? I always thought buildings – unlike ships – were genderless. Though come to think of it Kracklite always refers to buildings as masculine.

CASPASIAN: Like Boullée – he builds such aggressive buildings – that is when he builds them at all.

LOUISA: Whereas you . . .?

CASPASIAN: Certainly nothing higher than four storeys.

(*With a smile he makes a phallic gesture.*)

LOUISA: (*Looking out the window*) Then – we have – by the looks of it – reached your level . . .

(*The room is on the fourth floor.*)

They both move to the window and lean on the sill, looking out. Seen from behind – they make a symmetrical pair – the Augustan Mausoleum beyond them. CASPASIAN contrives to brush his leg against LOUISA's. Behind them – on the desk top – are Kracklite's Augustan stomachs. CASPASIAN puts his arm on LOUISA's waist and gradually drops it lower to her backside.

CASPASIAN: Every architect should know about shape and form and function and know what is proportionally strong . . . and enduring . . . and reliable.

LOUISA: (*Laughing*) . . . and cost-effective. (*Mocks him with architectural jargon.*) You're talking to an architect's wife.

CASPASIAN: I'd prefer to talk to an architect's mistress.

(*He stares at her face.*)

LOUISA: (*Smiling and removing his hand from her backside*) Jesus Christ, Caspasian – Kracklite was never *that* forward.

CASPASIAN: He was never *that* talented.

LOUISA: Or *that* arrogant. Still, you've taken your time. I've been in Rome now for over ten weeks . . . with your reputation

I'd have thought you would have made a move by now.

CASPASIAN: Maybe I was waiting for a sign from you?

LOUISA: What sign might that be?

CASPASIAN: (*Smiling*) Putting on a little weight – becoming more Roman . . . it's all right – I've guessed. Have you told him?

LOUISA: (*A little shamefaced*) No. I haven't.

CASPASIAN: Whyever not?

LOUISA: If you guessed I was pregnant – why couldn't he? (*She hangs her head.* CASPASIAN *kisses her forehead. She looks hard at him.*)

Do you always make passes at pregnant women?

CASPASIAN: (*Slyly and engagingly*) I always find pregnant women very attractive.

LOUISA leaves the window and moves towards the door – picking up her handbag from the bed. CASPASIAN takes up one of the Augustan stomachs.

CASPASIAN: May I keep one of these? – as a token . . . of a blossoming relationship?

LOUISA: Well, (*She smiles and nods*) I suggest that you don't let him know that you've taken it.

CASPASIAN takes out a pen and, aping Kracklite's method and staring flagrantly at LOUISA, he feels his groin, looks at his watch and then draws an erect phallus on the 'Augustan' photograph – leaning on the wall beside the door into the corridor all the time. Smiling, LOUISA opens the door into the corridor. CASPASIAN shows LOUISA the drawing.

LOUISA: Put it away

CASPASIAN: What?

LOUISA: The drawing . . . *and* the article.

LOUISA pulls CASPASIAN gently and provocatively out into the corridor. A few doors down the corridor, at a door that is ajar, a small boy – aged around eight – stands, wearing nothing except a white T-shirt – he watches CASPASIAN and LOUISA – LOUISA smiles at the boy. Then LOUISA and CASPASIAN walk away down the corridor. The boy watches them.

Section Fifteen: Afternoon, Friday, 2 August 1985

SCENE 25: THE BATHS AT THE VILLA ADRIANA

A wide 'architectural' panorama – the Baths of the Villa Adriana on a hot summer day. The image is finely composed, scrupulously lit – it's held for 15 seconds or more. Under one of the vaults of the Baths – dwarfed, and made to look insignificant – the 'Boullée' party sit for a picnic. They sit at a folding table under a large canvas parasol. IO SPECKLER has spared no expense. There are wicker baskets, wine bottles, fruit. Present are KRACKLITE, LOUISA, FLAVIA, CASPASIAN, IO, JULIO and FREDERICO.

CASPASIAN: (*Mainly for the benefit of entertaining* LOUISA) It is said that Hadrian – the man who built all this – was a man with a skin disease – who needed to keep his skin wet to stop him from scratching himself to pieces . . . hence the Baths. (*Indicates, with a flourish of his arm, the ruins about them.*) What he was obliged to suffer, others were persuaded to enjoy . . .

IO: Caspasian, you know that's not true.

CASPASIAN: It's a good story.

IO: Not good enough. You are talking about Caracalla. Hadrian was a genius, Caracalla merely a thug. Here at the Villa Adriana, Hadrian created modern architecture. (*Beginning to rhapsodize*) It is not unlikely that we are sitting in the seventh tepidarium . . . in four foot six inches of . . .

CASPASIAN: . . . tepid . . . and probably dirty water which almost certainly would not meet contemporary hygiene standards . . . (*Dismissively*) I'm sure it looks better as a ruin.

He's lying on his back with a sun hat over his eyes – he stretches and gets up and wanders away carrying a glass of wine.

IO: Rome in ruins has had more influence on architecture than it ever would brand new . . . what you can't see – you can imagine . . .

CASPASIAN: (*Shouting out before he disappears behind a column of masonry*) . . . sounds just like a woman with clothes on . . .

All this time, receiving food, KRACKLITE has been throwing it away, hopefully without attracting attention – throwing it over his shoulder, surreptitiously flicking it into the piled-up fragments of ruins, pilasters, capitals, mosaic sections, statue fragments. He takes some of the salami offered by FLAVIA and contrives to throw it behind the jumbled stones. In the shadow of some broken pillars, a lean, hungry dog has been devouring the scraps. Lured by the possibility of more – the dog makes an appearance. It rushes forward to grab food from the picnic table. The women scream.

LOUISA: Watch out – it's rabid!

KRACKLITE: (*Watching dispassionately*) Don't be hysterical.

IO: It certainly looks ill.

KRACKLITE: It's just hungry. Shoo it off.

LOUISA: It's your fault, Kracklite – throwing food into the bushes. (*Saunters off among the ruins. Calls back over her shoulder.*) If you don't want to eat – leave the food alone . . .

FLAVIA: It ought to be shot.

KRACKLITE: Would you shoot *anything* that looks ill?

FLAVIA: Now, Kracklite – are you looking for sympathy?

KRACKLITE: Shut up!

Feeling ill, KRACKLITE gets up, and watches the dog eat – then – as nonchalantly as he can, he disappears among the ruins.

SCENE 26: RUINS AT VILLA ADRIANA

KRACKLITE leans against a crumbling wall and vomits violently. He recovers – and wipes his mouth with his shirt-tails. The lean and hungry dog comes up to sniff at Kracklite's vomit . . . KRACKLITE watches it dispassionately . . . the dog eats the vomit.

SCENE 27: WRITING POSTCARD AT VILLA ADRIANA

KRACKLITE finds a spot of shade in the shadow of a ruined wall to sit down and write a postcard to Boullée.

Friday 2nd August 1985

Dear Etienne-Louis Boullée,
The pains are returning and I can't eat without vomiting.
If you breathe in and press your finger just to the right of your navel – can you feel a hard lump? Some days it's spherical, some days it

feels like a cube. Most days it feels like a sharp-cornered pyramid. I must have an old, old disease – did the Pharaohs suffer from stomach cramps? The Emperor Hadrian died of a perforated ulcer. When you're fifty-four and grateful for being able to sleep at night and eat badly and pee like a fire-engine – what do you do if you suspect your wife no longer cares for your company? – sorry, Etienne – since you never had a wife – that was never your problem. Maybe you were a sensible man.

Yours with respect,
St Kracklite

As he has been writing this, in the distance, CASPASIAN and LOUISA, walking hand in hand among the ruins, stop and sit in the grass beneath an olive tree. Their laughter attracts KRACKLITE's attention. He gets up from his seat on a stone wall and quietly watches them. He watches CASPASIAN put his arms around LOUISA.
With LOUISA's laughter still audible, the camera pans away from KRACKLITE's distraught face and frames a wide view and deep perspective of the ruins of the Villa Adriana . . . ready for –

Time-lapse 4
Accompanied by music that accentuates the 'raw' grandeur of the ruins, the sun slowly moves down into the evening sky; it sets, and the ruins are illuminated by floodlight. Night sets in, the floodlights are switched off one by one and the moon rises. The moon illuminates the ruins with a silver light.

Section Sixteen: Early Evening, Friday, 2 August 1985

SCENE 28: BATHROOM AND BEDROOM IN APARTMENT
There is a great swishing and splashing of water in the bath. Sprays of water splash on to the white marble floor tiles. The bath is very full – someone is drowning. It's KRACKLITE – he's not drowning – only pretending to. LOUISA, taking no notice of him whatsoever, is getting ready to go out to dinner. She walks about the suite – her hair wet. Kracklite's junk – his books and papers,

etc. – have been pushed to his side of the room. They are piled around his bed like a drift of rubbish. Exasperated, LOUISA finally agrees to take notice of KRACKLITE – which is what he wanted.

LOUISA: All right, Kracklite – what are you doing?

KRACKLITE: Drowning!

KRACKLITE continues to splash about – when LOUISA doesn't respond, he stops his splashing and surfaces, looking over the side of the bath at her. His hair is plastered to his forehead and water streams down his face. She continues to walk about the bedroom – passing and repassing the bathroom door – carrying nail varnish, a comb, a hair-dryer. KRACKLITE grimaces and, taking several pills from a bottle balanced on the side of the bath, swallows them with a mouthful of whisky from a tumbler also balanced on the side of the bath. Then he goes back to 'drowning' himself. Then he stops again – the bathwater gradually settles.

KRACKLITE: (*talking to himself so that* LOUISA *can hear*) It's no good. Your body just won't let you do it! Nobody every died by voluntarily ceasing to breathe. If you managed to stop breathing, you'd fall unconscious – and start breathing again . . .

LOUISA: (*Sitting on the bed, dressed in her underwear – her voice somewhat muffled as she bends over to trim her pubic hair*) You could try slashing your wrists.

KRACKLITE: True . . . it's appropriate in Rome.

LOUISA: You'll have to wait a moment – I'm using your razor.

KRACKLITE: (*Musing*) Livia was hairy.

LOUISA: (*Looking up with a spark of interest*) Who's she?

KRACKLITE: Augustus' wife.

LOUISA: How do you know she was hairy?

KRACKLITE: She used to leave hairs in the bath . . . it's in Caesar's *Gallic Wars* – Book Five – *she* tried to kill her husband.

LOUISA: With his razor?

KRACKLITE: No – figs. Poisoned figs.

LOUISA: I see.

KRACKLITE: He fell for it – according to Robert Graves.

LOUISA: (*Bored*) Who's he? An architect?

KRACKLITE: No – he was a mortuary attendant.

KRACKLITE lies back in his bath – with only his nose and mouth and belly above the water line. Then he sits up and looks into the bedroom – he can't see LOUISA.

KRACKLITE: Where are you going?

LOUISA: Caspasian and Flavia have invited me out to dinner.

KRACKLITE: Why didn't they ask me?

LOUISA: You can come if you like.

KRACKLITE: (*Petulantly*) I wasn't asked personally.

LOUISA appears around the door and looks stunning – dressed up, ready to go out. KRACKLITE momentarily forgets his complaining.

KRACKLITE: You look good . . . In fact, you look so good – I wouldn't be surprised if you were seeing Caspasian on his own.

LOUISA: Maybe I am.

KRACKLITE: I see.

LOUISA: (*Provocatively*) He knows how to treat women. He's young and he's entertaining.

KRACKLITE: So I noticed.

LOUISA: What do you mean?

KRACKLITE: I watched you in the Baths at Villa Adriana.
(*She is about to remonstrate*)
Don't worry – the location was very appropriate. You were continuing a tradition of nearly sixteen hundred years – the baths have always attracted whores and prostitutes.

LOUISA: (*Leaning seductively against the doorpost*) I'm pregnant.

KRACKLITE: (*After a pause*) You're what?

LOUISA comes into the bathroom and sits on the edge of the bath.

KRACKLITE: (*Disbelieving*) Are you sure?

LOUISA: Don't look so startled – it's yours.

KRACKLITE: (*Disbelieving*) When did it happen?

LOUISA: (*Angrily and sadly*) Stourley – how could you not have noticed? (*Defiantly*) Counting the weeks I'd say it was on the train to Rome.

KRACKLITE: But that's two months ago!

LOUISA: I'd say it was closer to three. You've hardly come near me since. (*Angrily and accusingly*) Your Boullée and your damn stomach aches are more important.

KRACKLITE: Are you sure this time?
(*She nods firmly and steadily.*) Which side of the border?
LOUISA: What?! (*After a moment's perplexity – and then laughing uproariously at his bizarre concern*) Why, I do believe it was the Italian side – just. (*Mock portentously*) But who can tell the moment of conception?
KRACKLITE: (*Musing, and stroking his belly*) I'm glad it's going to be an Italian child. Give me the towel. I'm coming with you.
LOUISA: You're not!
KRACKLITE: Oh? – and why not?

LOUISA, dressed and looking splendid, disregards his question and passes a large white towel to the naked and vulnerable wet-haired KRACKLITE, as he gets out of the bath. The contrast between her finely clothed appearance and his vulnerable nakedness is marked.

LOUISA: Aren't you pleased?
KRACKLITE: I couldn't be more pleased.
LOUISA: I'm not so sure you look it.
KRACKLITE: (*With a weak smile*) I'm very tired.
(*He's on the edge of tears – of happiness, relief, despair – a mixture of all three.*)

KRACKLITE gets out of the bath and goes into the bedroom – LOUISA follows – they sit on the bed. There is a silence. It's a pivotal moment for their reconciliation. Which is broken by the phone ringing. After it has rung several times KRACKLITE gets up to answer it.

LOUISA: Don't answer it – it'll be Caspasian. He's in the lobby.
KRACKLITE: I see.
LOUISA: Do you see?
(*She kicks off her shoes and takes off her jacket – the phone stops ringing.* KRACKLITE *picks it up and dials.*)
What are you doing?
KRACKLITE: (*Ringing the lobby*) This is room 424. Send up a bottle of champagne, and there is a Signor Speckler in the lobby – will you tell him that Signora Kracklite is indisposed and will contact him in the morning. Thank you. You are looking tired – we should celebrate with an early night – both of us.

(*He puts his hand on her belly and smiles.*)
Have you seen a doctor?
LOUISA: In a surgery overlooking the Colosseum? Like you?
KRACKLITE: (*Smiles wryly.*) I went to see him – with the same general area of anatomy in mind.
(*He strokes his belly.*)
LOUISA: And what did he say?
KRACKLITE: That it was overwork and overeating.
LOUISA: Did you believe him?
KRACKLITE: I believed him and then I didn't believe him. (*Sighs.*) As soon as this is over – let's go back to Chicago and take a long rest. (*Smiles thinly.*) Besides, I want to be the father of an American child. (*Leans back on the bed.*) God, I feel tired – it must be those pills.
LOUISA: Poor Kracklite.
(*She genuinely feels affection for him.*)

It seems that a weary reconciliation is possible. There is a knock at the door. LOUISA covers KRACKLITE with a sheet and leaves the bed to open the door to let in a waiter with a tray of glasses and the champagne.

LOUISA: Put it on the table. Will you open it for me, please?

He does so. LOUISA gives him a tip from her bag – three notes and then, when the waiter looks dissatisfied, a fourth. She returns to the bed to find KRACKLITE with his eyes closed. She gently shakes him and calls his name. He doesn't answer. She slaps his face – gently. He is sound asleep – he breathes deeply. She straightens up and stares at him. She pours herself a glass of champagne and sitting on the bed sips it, looking out of the window on to the Augustan Tomb. She is deep in thought. KRACKLITE is asleep, unexciting, familiar, he's totally wrapped up in his work and his illness. CASPASIAN is well, healthy, eager, promising, promiscuous and probably still waiting downstairs. The moment slips past – her relationship with her husband will by stages now slip away.

LOUISA gets off the bed and makes KRACKLITE more comfortable – plumping his pillow, pulling up the sheets and pulling over a blanket. She looks down at his sleeping face, and then, taking the phone with her, goes into the bathroom.

Through the ajar door, she can be seen making a phone call, sipping her champagne while she waits for a reply. She speaks quietly into the phone, masking her voice further by covering the mouthpiece with her hand.

LOUISA: Hello. This is Signora Kracklite. Is there anyone waiting for me? Yes . . . a Signor Speckler . . . Yes . . . Can you tell him to wait? I'll be down right away.

When she has finished, she drinks the rest of the champagne, puts on her shoes, puts on her jacket, turns out the bedside light. She goes into the bathroom and pulls out the bath plug. She turns out the bathroom light and the bathwater runs out in the gloom. We can hear the apartment door into the corridor click shut. The water gurgles quietly away, catching gleams of cold light.

Section Seventeen: Soon after Dawn on Saturday, 3 August 1985

SCENE 29: ST PETER'S

Time-lapse 5

From the close-up of the bathplug in the dark to a brilliant, early-morning time-lapse sunrise over St Peter's Square. An 'architectural' panorama – symmetrically composed and held for 20 seconds or more. Accompanied by a variation of the 'architectural' time-lapse music, the moon dims, the stars fade, the sky turns pink, the sun rises, the Dome glows orange, the shadows gradually shorten.

The exaggerated time reverts back, imperceptibly, into real time and KRACKLITE, looking tired and weary, stands before the Square, staring at St Peter's. In the foreground is a stone bench and KRACKLITE sits down – diminished by the setting. KRACKLITE sits glumly – one hand inside his waistband holding his stomach. He stares blankly at the distant St Peter's. He takes a bunch of gaudy postcards of views of Rome out of his jacket pocket – they are taken either at dusk or after nightfall. He selects one at random – it's a postcard of St Peter's, very similar to the view presently framed by the camera. He turns it over and writes on the back with a black ballpoint pen. First he writes the date. The address – in Paris – is already written. It's another postcard to Boullée.

Saturday 3 August 1985

Then, after a pause, he writes:

Dear Etienne-Louis Boullée,
I am apparently to be a father . . . were you ever a father . . . ?

He pauses, turns the card over, and idly accentuates the convex shape of the Colosseum with his pen – he turns the card upside down and continues to outline the shape. He stares at the Dome of St Peter's then turns the card over to the backside again and writes:

If your wife is unfaithful – how can you ever know if the child is really yours? My belly aches again. I had grapes for breakfast – was that wise?

A car pulls up at the kerb ten feet from him. In it is a grinning CASPASIAN. He opens the car door. FREDERICO, sitting in the front seat, gets out and squeezes himself in the back seat.

CASPASIAN: Signor Kracklite! Are you here for the religion or for the architecture? Let me drive you to the Gallery. Get in!

KRACKLITE finishes the card.

All the best.

Yours,
Stourley Kracklite

Against all his best inclinations, KRACKLITE gets up and approaches the nearby postbox. A man is leaning against the posting slot. KRACKLITE makes it obvious that he wants to post the card. The man stares into space and doesn't move. KRACKLITE gets the idea and gives him a coin. The man holds out his hand for the card – KRACKLITE hesitates and then gives it to him. The man looks at the address and then holds out his hand again – KRACKLITE gives him another coin – and then the man posts the card with a shrug and then resumes his position blocking the posting slot. KRACKLITE smiles at the man's cheek and walks over to CASPASIAN's car and gets in. The car drives off.

SCENE 30: CAR RIDE TO VITTORIANO

CASPASIAN drives fast under the arch at the top of the Piazza del Popolo and speeds across the piazza, darting between the two churches at the top of the Corso. Way down the end of the Corso, the Victor Emanuel Building gleams in the sun. They rapidly get closer and closer – the Emanuel Building grows larger and larger.

CASPASIAN: (*With a conspiratorial grin*) Frederico and I knew an irrepressible postcard writer, didn't we? He was always writing postcards to girls in America. He met a sticky end. He was studying American geography.

FREDERICO: He was sitting in the front passenger seat of his girlfriend's car on the way to the examination room . . .

CASPASIAN: . . . with a large heavy American atlas on his lap. His girlfriend was an erratic driver.

FREDERICO: She pulled up sharply at traffic lights . . .

CASPASIAN: . . . and wham! . . . the book went into his stomach.

CASPASIAN makes an extravagant gesture and slams the brakes on at a set of red traffic lights – KRACKLITE is thrown forward – he is startled, but unhurt. He contains his anger.

FREDERICO: (*With a smile at* KRACKLITE*'s discomfort*) Pages 67 and 68. The Nevada Desert was flooded with his blood . . .

CASPASIAN: . . . he always wanted to go to America . . . instead America came to him . . .

The car rushes out into the Piazza de Venezia, travels across the piazza and screeches to a halt by the steps of the Victor Emanuel. KRACKLITE slowly gets out.

KRACKLITE: (*Speaking slowly and with measured constraint through the car window to* CASPASIAN) You know, Caspasian, you're wasted in the architectural profession – you should have been a medical man – a doctor . . . (*With controlled vehemence*) It's quite difficult to build fakes, but it's easier to be a quack . . .

CASPASIAN drives away with a grin on his face – he narrowly misses KRACKLITE's feet. KRACKLITE stands still in the slipstream of the car – his hair and tie blowing in the wind. A wide shot sees KRACKLITE on the pavement outside the Vittoriano – a small diminutive figure.

Section Eighteen: Four in the Morning, Thursday, 22 August 1985

SCENE 31: VITTORIANO BASEMENT OFFICE
KRACKLITE is working late at night in his personal office in the subterranean room of the Vittoriano. His untidy working desk is illuminated in a bright pool of light in the gloom of the vast underground room. He is surrounded by plaster models of the Vittoriano sculpture. His desk is crowded with books and plans, papers and models, and postcard views of Rome. It is very quiet. Very noticeably – at the front of the desk – is a modest gyroscope – a toy – it lies on a scaled drawing of Boullée's spiral tower – the 'lighthouse tower'.
KRACKLITE stretches and immediately crumples up with pain. He takes out his bottle of pills, but finds no water with which to swallow them. Holding his stomach, he gets up and opens the door of his office into the building's atrium.

SCENE 32: VITTORIANO TOILET
The atrium is being prepared for the exhibition – it is shadowy and has the look of the Piranesi prisons etchings – ladders, hanging ropes, shrouded dustsheet sails.
KRACKLITE hurriedly crosses the atrium and up the stairs beyond. He (and we) hear voices (in Italian) and laughter . . . There is a streak of bright light issuing from the lavatories at the back of the first flight of stairs – it is the source of the voices – CASPASIAN and FREDERICO talking loudly. Swallowing his pain, KRACKLITE peers around the door of the lavatory.
CASPASIAN is in the act of passing over to FREDERICO a neat attaché case. He taps his nose for secrecy.

CASPASIAN: Here you are – 10 million lire. Officially – it's been credited to catering expenses. Bank it – we'll be able to make another deposit in a month. Kracklite will never know. Boullée will be doing us a service . . . and speaking of Boullée – I've found this . . . for Kracklite.

KRACKLITE – outside the lavatory door – in deep shadow – hears his name mentioned . . . he strains to catch what they are saying – the pain in his stomach is still intense – he is caught between staying outside to listen and entering to get a drink of water to swallow his pills.

CASPASIAN takes a folder and opens it – shows FREDERICO an engraving. We can see the engraving but KRACKLITE cannot. It pictures an eighteenth-century figure in full wig and armour, carrying a roll of plans and a set-square, and seems to represent Architecture.

FREDERICO: It's even got his paunch . . .

CASPASIAN: You can sell it to him as a fair likeness of his hero. (FREDERICO *and* CASPASIAN *laugh derisively.* CASPASIAN *looks at his watch.*)

And now I have . . . (*Taps his nose and ironically rolls his eyes*) . . . an assignation . . . with a lady who eats cake.

KRACKLITE makes to step inside the lavatory. At the same time FREDERICO sees CASPASIAN out of the lavatory by a door opposite.

KRACKLITE enters the lavatory and hurriedly fills his glass at the tap – he swallows his pills and stands momentarily at the basin, waiting for relief. He slumps down on the wooden bench vacated by CASPASIAN. For a moment he notices nothing – intent on his pain – then he sees Frederico's attaché case left on the bench with Frederico's raincoat, the folder left by Caspasian and a roll of plans. The case is not locked. As relief comes, KRACKLITE relaxes and, curious as to the contents of the case and the meaning of the secrecy, opens the attaché case – it is full of American banknotes. As KRACKLITE stares at the money and flicks through a bundle of notes, FREDERICO returns and is startled to see KRACKLITE – he recovers quickly.

FREDERICO: What are you doing, Kracklite – looking in my personal property?

KRACKLITE: For a start – wondering where you got a suitcase

full of American dollars?

FREDERICO: (*Somewhat sheepishly*) It's to pay for the models...

KRACKLITE: It seems a great deal of money. And how come you are handling the money personally?

FREDERICO: The assistants want to be paid in cash... (*Sheepishly*) And I still haven't been paid for the cake...

KRACKLITE: I could get those models for half the price in Chicago. Where is the model of Boullée's lighthouse? It should have been ready three weeks ago.

FREDERICO: It's fine... fine!

(*He looks guilty*.)

KRACKLITE: Can I see it?... Do you have it upstairs now?

FREDERICO: Not now, Kracklite – it's late – I have to go... Caspasian has taken it... to show you... he's taken it to your apartment... Look – he's asked me to give you this.

FREDERICO, eager to divert KRACKLITE, picks up the file Caspasian gave him and produces the engraving of the figure of Architecture. The abdomen of the statue in the engraving is noticeably articulated.

FREDERICO: It's Boullée.

KRACKLITE: (*Interested*) What makes you think it's Boullée?... It's just a figure representing Architecture... There are no likenesses of Boullée – I should know – I've been searching for one for ten years.

FREDERICO: You must ask Caspasian for the details... look, the inscription's French and the date is correct... Caspasian found it at the Bibliothèque Nationale.

KRACKLITE: (*Shouting*) That doesn't prove it's Boullée! (*His voice echoes in the hall outside*.)

There is the sound of double footsteps outside in the passage – KRACKLITE and FREDERICO hold up their heads to listen. There is a jangle of keys and FLAVIA puts her head around the door, closely followed by IO – who is holding her arm. They are both wearing raincoats and have just come in from the rain.

FLAVIA: What 'doesn't prove it's Boullée'?

KRACKLITE: His picture being in the Bibliothèque Nationale.

IO: Good evening, gentlemen... working late?

FLAVIA: (*Indicating the engraving*) Let me have a look. (*Peers closely at the engraving.*) He's wearing a toga romana . . . and (*Laughing.*) I do believe lace-up shoes.

FREDERICO: By the expression on his face . . . it looks as though his shoes were pinching his feet . . .

FLAVIA: No . . . he's just eaten something nasty . . .

FREDERICO: I'm afraid it's worse than that . . .

FLAVIA:Yep! . . . disease of the pancreas!

FREDERICO: Pancreatic carcinoma!

IO: Sounds like a pasta eaten at Bolzano.

KRACKLITE: (*Worried – and not fully aware that they are stringing him along*) Who said Boullée died of cancer?

FLAVIA: Stourley! – for God's sake – don't be stupid – we're joking!

FREDERICO: (*Laughing*) I'm just on my way out. (*To* FLAVIA) I'll give you a lift.

FREDERICO picks up his attaché case and other belongings and he and FLAVIA leave by the same door FLAVIA came in. IO switches off the lights and he and KRACKLITE follow FREDERICO and FLAVIA out.

SCENE 33: VITTORIANO ATRIUM

With FREDERICO and FLAVIA some way down the atrium ahead of them, IO and KRACKLITE walk down the atrium stairs – back to Kracklite's office.

IO: What have you still got to do?

KRACKLITE: The main gallery hasn't even been started because of the hold-up on the Newton model – we're having to pay the electricians to stand by otherwise we'll lose them . . .

They both walk in the echoic empty spaces of the Gallery. IO switching off the lights as they go. FREDERICO and FLAVIA have turned off by a side entrance – they shout an echoic good night.

SCENE 34: VITTORIANO BASEMENT OFFICE

They arrive at Kracklite's office – KRACKLITE collects his papers, briefcase, maps, plans, memos, telephone messages – they switch out the lights. KRACKLITE still carries the medicine glass.

IO: (*Indicating the glass in* KRACKLITE*'s hand*) Are you feeling any better?

KRACKLITE: No. (*Belches.*) I've been asked to believe it's only constipation, but it's been going on far too long for that now . . . I can't believe that any more. (*Wearily – and with unconvincing nonchalance*) I expect it's just overwork . . .

IO: Why don't you take some time off?

KRACKLITE: No – I wouldn't hear of it.

IO: We could delay the opening date . . .

KRACKLITE: (*Heatedly*) No! – That's just what we can't do!

IO: Then offload some of the responsibility. Give it to Caspasian . . . he can take care of the details for a few weeks . . .

KRACKLITE: (*Almost to himself*) That's what I'm frightened of . . .

IO: He's capable enough.

There is a silence for a few moments. The last thing KRACKLITE picks up off his desk is the toy gyroscope – he puts it in his pocket – they make to leave.

KRACKLITE: No. (*Quietly*) He's taken over too much of my life already.

IO switches off the lights and they leave by walking down the broad underground corridor, switching off the lights as they go.

SCENE 35: VITTORIANO MAIN HALL

The Newton Room is lit with shadowy, criss-crossed, artificial light. It is a huge space – Piranesi-like. In preparation for the Exhibition – shrouded objects look ambiguous – there is a very large blow-up engraving of the Colosseum unrolled on the floor. IO and KRACKLITE emerge from the back of the huge room as tiny figures. The large window above the balcony – letting in muted dawn light – has also been letting in the rain. There are several buckets on the floor to catch the drips. One is very full. KRACKLITE moves the full bucket to replace it with an empty one. The falling drips echo in the large space. KRACKLITE is excessively loaded with rolled plans, books, folders and a briefcase. He approaches the photocopying machine – the same one as before, but now with a new home. He switches it on and it illuminates his face with green light. He puts down most of his load and begins to feed the engraving of Boullée given to him by FREDERICO into the enlarging machine.

KRACKLITE: (*His own marital problems uppermost in his mind*) Let me ask you an impertinent question.

IO: (*With a laugh*) Go on.

KRACKLITE: Why did you divorce your wife?

IO: (*With a smile that shows he's understood why* KRACKLITE *has asked the question*) Ah–ah! Jealousy!

The blow-up stomachs of the Boullée engraving emerge from the photocopier.

KRACKLITE begins to collect up the dozen photocopied blow-ups.

KRACKLITE: And was your jealousy well founded?

IO: I thought so at the time . . . Now I am not so sure. But . . . the damage was done. Too much had been said, too much vengeance taken. She now lives in Paris – and you will be amused by this – she lives at Number 7 Rue Reaumur in the Quai d'Anise . . .

(KRACKLITE *is visibly surprised.*)

. . . the only building left in Paris that was built by Boullée.

IO smiles. He switches off the photocopier. KRACKLITE picks up his many belongings. IO switches off most of the Newton Room lights – the vast room becomes a more and more mysterious space, in virtual darkness.

IO opens the huge door on to the outside. It lets in a blaze of light – it is dawn over Rome – the heavy rain of the night has stopped and the sky is virtually cloudless though the marble of the building – the stairs, steps and terraces gleam with the recent rain. IO and KRACKLITE are dwarfed figures against the sunlight.

IO: Look . . . if you won't take time off – at least come to the Baths at Trento with us one Sunday. It'll do you good.

KRACKLITE: When things slacken off later – I might.

IO: I'll bring Trettorio – you can ask him learned questions about ancient medicine and prompt him for a diagnosis.

They walk out into the sunlight, down the steps. IO waves and turns off to the right. KRACKLITE – heavily laden with his belongings – walks off to the left. The camera observes the view of Rome.

Section Nineteen: Just after Dawn, Thursday, 22 August 1985

SCENE 36: KRACKLITE'S APARTMENT HALLWAY

KRACKLITE travels up in the apartment lift – the lights flick and fleck his head and shoulders.

Coming out of the lift into the hotel corridor, KRACKLITE, looking very tired, walks towards his suite – it's early morning – the early-morning sun patterning the corridor with bars of low light and long shadows. KRACKLITE carries his briefcase, the early-morning papers and an ill-assorted collection of maps, charts and papers, and the photocopies of Boullée. Passing Room 412 (some eight doors away from his own suite at Number 424), he hears laughter – female laughter which he is sure he recognizes – he hesitates. He walks back a pace, looks up and down the corridor, hesitates – then bends down and looks through the keyhole.

Through the keyhole – he sees into a room of light and dark contrasts. LOUISA is sitting on a red-corded black couch. We see enough to know that the lower part of her body is naked. CASPASIAN – naked, but with his trousers and pants around his ankles – is leaning over the back of the couch. They are laughing. KRACKLITE is crushed. And fascinated. From a bent-over, crouching position outside the door – without thinking and totally absorbed – he moves his cramped leg to a more comfortable position and goes down into a kneeling stance – his eye fixed to the keyhole. He looks like an abject penitent.

Inside the room – LOUISA has rolled off the couch and, on all fours, is crawling around to the back – away from KRACKLITE's sight. Largely obscured by the couch – the couple meet at the far end of it. CASPASIAN stands over LOUISA.

Breathless and white-faced, KRACKLITE, in the corridor – without taking his eye from the keyhole – reaches out for a chair placed beside the door. He pulls it up behind him and eases himself backwards into it. It scratches and screeches on the parquet flooring. It creaks under his bulk. He doesn't take his eyes from the keyhole. Behind him and up the corridor, a door opens. A CHILD looks out and watches KRACKLITE – it's the same child as we saw earlier. The BOY has wet hair and he is draped in a large white towel. He has slippers on – it's apparent that he's just had a bath. He carries a large bright orange.

In the contrasting dark and light areas of the hotel room – LOUISA and CASPASIAN move out of the couch area, through an area of bright light into the bedroom beyond. CASPASIAN walks like a duck – his ankles are still hampered by his fallen trousers. They are laughing.

KRACKLITE, with tears beginning to run down his face, rests his head on the door. The CHILD up the corridor watches.

From the room behind the CHILD, a WOMAN's voice:

WOMAN: (*In Italian*) What are you doing?

CHILD: (*In Italian*) I'm watching a man crying.

WOMAN: (*In Italian*) What's he crying for?

Through the keyhole of the hotel room, KRACKLITE watches CASPASIAN come out of the bedroom. His ankles are no longer hampered by his trousers. He is carrying a neat architectural model of a building with a tower – it's the model of Boullée's 'Truncated Cone-shaped Tower'. It's the lighthouse referred to earlier. The way that Caspasian carries the model, it hides (and substitutes) his genitals. He puts it down on the small table in front of the couch where it stands in a shaft of sunlight. CASPASIAN returns to the bedroom.

KRACKLITE crumples up outside the door. He half leans his weight – his head and shoulders – on to the door frame. His left cheek is pushed up against the door knob. His suit is crushed and the chair slides forward on two legs. The CHILD watches him.

CHILD: (*In English*) What are you crying for?

KRACKLITE: (*Without moving his body – but looking at the* CHILD) There's a draught through the keyhole and it's making my eyes water.

WOMAN: (*Her voice just audible from the room behind the* CHILD, *in Italian*) What's the man crying for?

CHILD: (*In Italian*) He's got a draught in his eyes.

KRACKLITE nods quietly . . . and the small movement causes the chair to collapse – spilling him on the floor. The CHILD – coping with the large bath towel – hurries over to help him up. KRACKLITE's papers have gone all over the floor – including the photocopies of the Boullée stomach. The CHILD looks at one of the Boullée stomachs and, taking one without Kracklite seeing him, he secretes it under the corridor carpet. KRACKLITE puts a finger to his lips and whispers 'Ssshh'. The man and the CHILD tiptoe exaggeratedly about, picking up the papers and the pieces of the chair. They stack the chair pieces neatly against the corridor wall.

When the job is finished, KRACKLITE and the BOY stare at one another. Then the BOY gives KRACKLITE his orange.

KRACKLITE takes it and, feeling the toy gyroscope in his pocket, takes it out and gives it to the BOY.

The WOMAN whose voice we have just heard comes to the head of the corridor to watch. The sunlight backlights her hair – she is very beautiful. With the pieces stacked, the CHILD returns to his mother. After having handled the large towel with some skill, he is now beaten by it and it falls to the floor. Mother and naked child stand in the sunlit doorway – they resemble a Raphael Madonna and Child. KRACKLITE stares at them for a moment, then nods his thanks and, backing away, walks back down the flight of steps where he entered the building. He occasionally turns and looks over his shoulder.

When KRACKLITE has gone, the CHILD crosses the landing carpet and looks through the vacated keyhole.

The CHILD sees only an empty room – shafted with sunlight – the model of the tower symmetrically placed in a beam of bright sun.

Section Twenty: Early Morning, Thursday, 22 August 1985

SCENE 37: THE ROMAN FORUM

Time-lapse 6

The sun rises in exaggerated time over an architectural view of the Forum from the Palatine Hill looking north toward the Arch of Titus and the Colosseum beyond. The low, early-morning mist partly obscuring the buildings and trees fades and disperses. The long shadows shorten. The shot runs some 20 seconds or more and is accompanied by the 'architectural' time-lapse music-material.

As exaggerated time imperceptibly changes to real time – the music retreats – and into the shot – in the foreground – KRACKLITE appears. His forehead is smudged, his eyes are red, his collar is undone. He stares at the view and sits on the parapet. In the distance is an ambiguous sound – like someone possibly knocking stone with a hammer. He takes out a wad of coloured postcards from his inside jacket pocket – they are already addressed with the Paris address our attention has been drawn to before. He then takes out a fountain pen which he carefully unscrews. He bites deep into the orange he has been carrying, given to him by the small boy. The juice spurts over his shirt. He takes no notice. He writes almost absent-mindedly. Writing to Boullée has always comforted him – but he scarcely knows now what he writes.

August 22nd 1985

Dear Etienne-Louis,
Did you ever come to Rome? . . . did you ever eat an orange . . . do you know what vitamin C can do for you . . . ? It's supposed to make you healthy.

The background noise of the hammer on stone, now closer, rouses KRACKLITE's attention. He listens and then gets up to investigate. He carries his orange and postcards.
In the early-morning light to the north of the Capitoline, a man is knocking the nose off a statue – he is using a small tack hammer. He carries a black plastic bag. KRACKLITE approaches him and watches him. He is a man with a lugubrious expression. Neither speaks. The nose collector knows that KRACKLITE is there but – after a cursory look – takes no notice of him. When the nose is off, the MAN puts it in his plastic bag and moves on to the next statue.

KRACKLITE, moving with the MAN, is handed the plastic bag to hold while the nose collector begins to chip at the face of a bald senator. KRACKLITE looks inside the bag – it is full of stone noses.

MAN: (*In Italian*) Is there something I can do for you?

KRACKLITE: I'm sorry – I don't speak much Italian . . . (*After a pause*) Do you mind if I watch?

KRACKLITE doesn't speak Italian – but his gestures and arm movements indicate the question perfectly well. The nose chipper smiles and shrugs and graciously allows him to watch. He shifts his hammer to his other hand, looks up and down the terrace garden and resumes chipping. KRACKLITE runs his hand over the statue's belly.

The MAN stops chipping, takes out a large and rather dirty handkerchief and blows his nose. Absolutely no connection is forged or looked for by the MAN or KRACKLITE – it seems a normal thing to do. The MAN resumes chipping and the nose comes off. The MAN puts the nose in his bag and moves off to the next statue.

KRACKLITE turns to the northward-looking view of the Forum, overlooking the Foro Traiano. He resumes his postcard writing:

. . . Etienne-Louis, what was the current stomach complaint when you were alive . . . ? gallstones? . . . kidney stones? . . . excess bile? . . . pancreatic carcinoma? . . . or is that a pasta eaten at Bolzano?

KRACKLITE looks up at the sun rising above the mist, illuminating the buildings of Rome. Tears smudge his face.

Section Twenty-one: Afternoon, Sunday, 29 September 1985

SCENE 38: PUBLIC BATHS STEAM ROOM

At a spa outside Rome – a large, echoic collection of marble halls – a trifle gloomy, full of tepid pools, long perspectives, statuary, steam, big and small spaces and a 'Sunday' crowd of bathers. IO, JULIO, KRACKLITE and TRETTORIO (the Doctor of Ancient Medicine we met at the Opening of the Gallery) walk towards camera. Bathers – men, in many different stages of undress – pass continually between them and us. The scene is ageless – thanks to the marble and the nakedness, both of which refuse to pin down the date – it could be Roman, Renaissance or modern. Only very close inspection would reveal modern plumbing. The location conjures up a possible vision of how the Baths at the Villa Adriana might have looked. A large proportion of the male visitors are middle-aged and overweight. IO, JULIO and TRETTORIO find little novelty in the situation, though KRACKLITE is ever watchful. He is especially curious about men his own weight and age.

KRACKLITE: God! . . . there's no cause for vanity here! – there are no distinctions – everyone's anonymous!

TRETTORIO: Don't you believe it! Far from it! They are all nakedly identified! He's a butcher.

(KRACKLITE *looks hard at the passing bathers to see if he can see a visual clue – he sees large hands.*)

He's a schoolteacher.

(KRACKLITE *sees steamed-up glasses.*)

He sells tobacco.

(KRACKLITE *sees nicotine-stained fingers.*)

And he sells motorcyles.

(KRACKLITE *sees bow legs.*)

KRACKLITE: How can you tell?

TRETTORIO: (*With a smile, and not answering the question*) He's got eight children.

(KRACKLITE *sees large genitals.*)

He's a banker.

(KRACKLITE *sees a large backside.*)

He's a Communist.

(KRACKLITE *sees a reddened back.*)

And he's a zoologist.

(KRACKLITE *sees a hairy chest. He always looks for the obvious – the stereotype.*)

KRACKLITE: (*Exasperated, and provocative*) Find me an architect!

Amused, they all look for a likely candidate for an architect. They see flat feet, melancholic eyes, pigeon chests, squints, and an excess of paunches.

TRETTORIO: (*With a laugh*) There aren't too many of them

about.

KRACKLITE. I don't know how the hell you could tell.

TRETTORIO: (*Laughing*) Medical Records!

KRACKLITE: They're your patients!?

TRETTORIO: Some of them.

KRACKLITE: Why don't they acknowledge you?

TRETTORIO: I'm the last person they'd want to acknowledge in public – though it's good to see them taking my advice.

SCENE 39: PUBLIC BATHS FRESCO ROOM

The four men are sitting in a painted room. They are wrapped in large white towels – JULIO with the towel around his head, Seneca-like, looking like a shrouded monk – IO wrapped about the shoulders looking like a dignified Roman senator, TRETTORIO with the towel around his waist, and KRACKLITE, nearly naked – identifying most with the naked mythological figures around the painted walls – the most timeless and heroic figure. They are sitting on a stone bench. Frescos of watery mythology cover the walls. On the ceiling is painted the death of Phaethon – an allegory of hubris and gravity. The company are drinking spa-water out of Russian-style glasses – silver spoons and silver-metal rims. They look like four Roman sages of an unspecified allegorical significance. KRACKLITE's attention is taken by the (prophetic) subject matter of the walls. After a silence, TRETTORIO speaks.

TRETTORIO: Signor Kracklite – do you dream?

KRACKLITE: Yes.

TRETTORIO: What do you dream of?

KRACKLITE: Recently – stairs. I'm forever climbing stairs. (*More quietly*) And falling down stairs.

(KRACKLITE *looks at Phaethon falling out of the sky*.) → don't like this now

TRETTORIO: A sure sign of dyspepsia.

KRACKLITE: No – I don't believe that any more.

TRETTORIO: Then what do you believe?

(KRACKLITE *looks at the fresco of the aged naked Neptune*.)

KRACKLITE: Boullée died of cancer.

TRETTORIO: Your respect for the man, Kracklite, does not imply that you have to suffer his complaints.

IO: Monsieur Boullée was a French hypochondriac – did you know that?
(KRACKLITE *shakes his head.*)
TRETTORIO: He was a little lame – are you a little lame?
KRACKLITE: (*Unsure*) No.
IO: He suffered from gout . . .
(KRACKLITE *looks at the fresco of Jupiter hurling a thunderbolt at Phaethon.*)
TRETTORIO: . . . he was frightened of thunderstorms – they made him incontinent . . .

They laugh – KRACKLITE does not join in. We are not absolutely sure – like KRACKLITE – whether they are telling the truth or inventing in an attempt to dispel KRACKLITE's fears or to mock his self-pity and hypochondria. KRACKLITE stares at the frescos.

KRACKLITE: (*Sadly*) You seem well informed.
IO: (*Joking*) Why do you think he built so little?
TRETTORIO: Why do you think he travelled so little?
IO: His illness incapacitated him.
TRETTORIO: He stayed at home for fear of embarrassment abroad.
(KRACKLITE *ignores their jibes – he stares sadly at the frescos.*)

The scene is shadowy. Stripes of sunlight filter through from unseen windows.

TRETTORIO: (*Realizing that* KRACKLITE *can't take the joking*) Look, Kracklite – I can't examine you here – but if you're worried – I'll make an appointment for you with my cousin for next week. He is a stomach specialist – he specializes in the guts of priests. (*With a smile*) Did you know that the average human intestine is twenty-seven feet long but that of a priest is three feet longer?
IO: On account of the indigestible Consecrated Host?
TRETTORIO: No. Much simpler. 'The Lord moves in mysterious ways, his duties to perform.'
(*They all laugh.*)
Look! There's one!
JULIO: Where?
KRACKLITE: One what?
TRETTORIO: An architect!

They all peer through the shadows. They see an obese man with a squint, a naked man covering his head with a towel, a thin bearded man on silver crutches, a red-faced man coughing hard . . . and CASPASIAN. He is standing in front of a full-length mirror, carefully combing his wet hair in front of his steamy reflection.

KRACKLITE: (*Almost to himself*) Jesus Christ! . . . it would be!

Section Twenty-two: Late Afternoon, Sunday, 29 September 1985

SCENE 40: POSTCARDS IN APARTMENT LIFT

KRACKLITE enters the apartment lift. Before he can shut the gates, the eight-year-old BOY we've met before steps into it. KRACKLITE pushes the floor button and they ascend in silence. The CHILD is carrying the large key to his mother's suite of rooms. Man and child secretly watch one another. KRACKLITE – as always – is carrying a great deal – books, papers – and this time a wet towel from the Spa Baths. His hair is wet. He coughs and moves his arm . . . and drops a bundle of coloured postcards of Rome that scatter all over the lift floor. The CHILD helps him pick them up.

KRACKLITE: Do you collect postcards?

BOY: No.

KRACKLITE. These are *all* of Rome.

They both kneel on the floor of the carpeted lift, picking up the cards.

KRACKLITE: These stretch right across the city. Look, if you start here (*Shows him a card of the Piazza del Popolo*) you can get right across Rome to the Appian Way – step by step – from this one you can see the next one and so on.

KRACKLITE demonstrates with a succession of cards. The lift arrives at their floor – but they continue to sit on the floor of the lift.

KRACKLITE: Pretty good, eh? It's about the only city you can do it with. I'm sending them to my friend in Paris – it's said that he's never been to Rome – it'll help him find his way around. He died in 1799 – that's nearly two hundred years ago – that's a long time – though Rome hasn't changed that much. Do I smell funny?

(*He sniffs his armpits.*)

BOY: Yes.

KRACKLITE: It's the smell of death, I reckon.

BOY: Is that why I saw you crying the other day?

KRACKLITE: Oh no – that was just practising.

BOY: Practising?

KRACKLITE: Yes . . . for an onion-peeling competition.

BOY: Oh?

The lift gates open and two astonished guests find KRACKLITE and the BOY sitting at ease on the floor – their backs against the lift wall and their legs outstretched – the postcards spread out before them. KRACKLITE and the BOY look up – blinking in the sudden bright lights.

Section Twenty-three: Afternoon, Tuesday, 3 December 1985

SCENE 41: HOSPITAL

KRACKLITE is at the hospital. He is waiting in a small side room for his medical examination. The room is full of sunlight – it's white and bright – with elegant medical trolleys and furniture – chrome, glass and black leather. There are one or two medical instruments – like some lengths of rubber tubing coiled in a glass tray. KRACKLITE – wearing a white dressing-gown – paces the room. He has a postcard of the Forum, and his fountain-pen, in his hand. He leans on the wall and writes on the postcard – it's already dated:

Tuesday 3rd December 1985

Dear Etienne,

I don't like doctors . . . they always see you at a disadvantage . . . when they have pored over your private parts, smelt your breath, fingered your tongue . . . how can you talk with them as an equal . . . ?

He idly takes up the rubber tubing, and puts down his postcard and pen. He measures the length of the rubber tubing for yardage, stretching it from the tip of his nose to the end of his outstretched arm. He measures out nine lengths – 9 yards – 27 feet. He then winds it tightly into folds and coils and measures it against his belly, seeing for himself what twenty-seven feet of intestine would represent. The doctor, ARTUSO AMANSA, watches him ironically from the doorway.

AMANSA: Signor Kracklite – are you ready?

KRACKLITE nods and a little sheepishly puts down the tubing. Two orderlies and a nurse enter. KRACKLITE gets on to the stretcher trolley and, accompanied by the nurse, the doctor and the two orderlies, he is wheeled out into the wide corridor. Back in the room, the postcard has been left half written . . .

Out in the corridor, coming up alongside KRACKLITE's little procession is another – similarly accompanied – and the patient – lying flat on his back and apparently unconscious – is the elderly SALVATORE BATTISTINO – the Secretary of the Society – he is arrayed around with saline drips, blood drips, tubes in his mouth and nostrils – he looks very white and close to death. The two processions stop at an intercrossing of corridors and KRACKLITE sits up and recognizes BATTISTINO. The orderlies accompanying the two trolleys talk together in Italian – and a doctor feels BATTISTINO's pulse and indicates to an orderly to pull a sheet over him. Before KRACKLITE can react or comment, he is moved swiftly away – he strains to look back.

KRACKLITE is lying on a hospital pallet in a small 'operating room'. There are a nurse and two assistants in the room, which contains glass-fronted medical cabinets full of instruments, various imposing pieces of computer-controlled equipment and a TV monitor. An anaesthetist is taking a needle out of KRACKLITE's arm. The doctor AMANSA is standing over KRACKLITE.

AMANSA: Now, Signor Kracklite, would you please lie on your left side – and bend your knees. I trust you know what we intend doing – it will be a little uncomfortable, but with the anaesthetic, you will feel very little. We intend examining the intestine with this probe. (*Shows* KRACKLITE *an instrument attached to a length of thin red-rubber tubing – it's very long.*) With an optical light source, we can take a small television camera into the large intestine and take live pictures that will appear on that television monitor there (*Points*) – this way – we can search for irregularities. We will make our full report and then ask you to come back.

They proceed. KRACKLITE watches the black-and-white TV monitor. He watches a picture of his own insides. The camera moves slowly through the cavernous intestines. KRACKLITE stares, half conscious. The doctor and his assistants also watch the monitor. With the image of his own bowels before him, KRACKLITE falls unconscious.

Section Twenty-four: Afternoon, Tuesday, 3 December 1985

SCENE 42: CASPASIAN'S ROOM IN IO'S HOUSE

Afternoon bright light floods across a bedroom. Mirrors, crisp white sheets. Dark shadowy spaces. On the bed, LOUISA and CASPASIAN. LOUISA lies on her left side with her back to camera – the same position as KRACKLITE in the last scene. CASPASIAN strokes LOUISA's belly with the back of his hand. They have been enjoying a late siesta together.

CASPASIAN: Do you know what I would like to do?

LOUISA: (*With a laugh*) No.

CASPASIAN: I would like to take him out . . . and put mine in his place.

LOUISA: (*Laughing*) Are you really jealous?

CASPASIAN: Yes . . . imagine the poor bastard . . .

LOUISA: He's no bastard . . . (*With an affectionate laugh*) Yours would be the bastard!

CASPASIAN: All right – the little 'legitimate' will have Kracklite's pudgy face and Kracklite's short arms and Kracklite's clumsy feet.

LOUISA: (*Sarcastically and amused*) Whereas yours?

CASPASIAN: *Ours*. For a start – *he* will be a girl.

LOUISA: (*Laughing*) Some sort of hermaphrodite?
CASPASIAN: *She* will have my black hair and your voice. She will be built the way you are – well . . . maybe a fuller mouth . . . and less hair on her private parts . . .
LOUISA: Careful! Your criticisms do not go unnoticed.
CASPASIAN: You look beautiful pregnant . . . like I said you would – my sister would like to photograph you . . .
LOUISA: Who for?
CASPASIAN: For you . . . for her . . . for me . . .
LOUISA: And for Kracklite?
CASPASIAN: Perhaps . . . would you do it?
LOUISA: No.
CASPASIAN: And whyever not?
LOUISA: Your sister worries me. She is *more* predatory than you.
CASPASIAN: (*Laughing*) Really?
LOUISA: (*Laughing in return*) I'm sure *she's* hermaphrodite.
CASPASIAN: I can assure you that she isn't.
LOUISA: How do you know?
CASPASIAN: She *is* my sister – we used to bathe together.
LOUISA: (*Laughing*) That was a long time ago.
CASPASIAN: Is last Tuesday a long time ago?
LOUISA: What!
CASPASIAN: I was joking. You know you look beautiful when you are shocked.
LOUISA: (*Smiling*) You only look beautiful when you are asleep and not scheming or planning or manipulating.
CASPASIAN: (*Mock surprise*) Me?!
LOUISA: (*With a long sigh*) However . . . if he or you were to be the father – what difference would it make? The child would always be the child of an architect.
CASPASIAN: At least with me – it would *not* be posthumously!
LOUISA: What do you mean?
CASPASIAN: The way Kracklite is going – he won't last until summer.
LOUISA: (*Playfully – but with significance*) Are you planning to kill him?
CASPASIAN: (*With return iciness*) I was convinced that was what you were doing!

LOUISA: (*Continuing the playful game*) And what would I gain?
CASPASIAN: The best motive is always freedom. I don't think either of us have to do anything illegal to gain your freedom. We just watch.

Section Twenty-five: Late Afternoon, Tuesday, 3 December 1985

SCENE 43: HOSPITAL

Back in the surgical review room. It is more 'shaded' than last time. Some of the lights have been turned down while KRACKLITE recovers from the anaesthetic. Most of the light falls on the large, inert form of KRACKLITE lying on the pallet. An assistant is seated in the far corner of the room – writing.
Around KRACKLITE – the equipment hums . . . he brings to mind a stranded whale . . . isolated . . . beached . . . in an alien environment.
On the TV screen – in black and white – is a programme about architecture . . . Roman (baroque) architecture. Slowly moving cameras pass along colonnades, down 'tunnels' of marble decoration . . . accompanied by an ornate Italian dialogue soundtrack . . . and sonorous music.
The slowly moving architectural footage recalls the footage of the 'journey' down KRACKLITE's intestines.

Section Twenty-six: Morning, Monday, 20 January 1986

SCENE 44: PIAZZA NAVONA

Time-lapse 7
Accompanied by the time-lapse 'Architectural' music the sun rises in exaggerated time over the Piazza Navona. The shadows form and shorten – the square is filled with early-morning orange light.

Imperceptibly, real time takes over and KRACKLITE is revealed, trying to photograph the belly of a male nude in the Bernini fountain – a mass of flying baroque sculpture and falling water. FLAVIA approaches silently. She watches KRACKLITE with amusement.

FLAVIA: And why aren't you working this morning, Kracklite?

KRACKLITE turns round but doesn't react with any surprise at seeing FLAVIA. He doesn't reply to her question, but returns to photographing. FLAVIA smiles and tries a different line of questioning.

FLAVIA: Tell me, Kracklite . . . why don't you photograph women?

KRACKLITE: (*Grumpily*) Different metabolism! Different shape, different organs, different complaints!

FLAVIA: (*Trying a different tack*) Have you eaten? Don't take the photos into the light – you'll miss the details.

KRACKLITE: (*With mock politeness*) Thank you. Are you giving advice?

FLAVIA: If you buy me a meal – I'll take the photos for you. (*She reaches out her hand for the camera – he passes it over.*) Are you interested just in the cocks?
(*She provocatively moves in close to a male statue.*)

KRACKLITE: No – I'm interested in the bellies.
(*His obsessions absorb her sexual provocation.*)

FLAVIA. A new erogenous zone?

KRACKLITE: Bellies were the *most* erogenous zone in the thirteenth century.

FLAVIA. (*Provocatively*) Really? On men?

KRACKLITE: (*Attempting a return sexual provocation*) Is your navel shaped like that?
(*He points at a navel.*)

FLAVIA: (*Not answering*) For this one – (*Clicks the camera*) I want avocado vinaigrette . . . and this one (*Clicks again*) insalata tricolore, and for this one (*Clicks*) scallopina marsala . . . with asparagus . . . and this one (*Click*) frangipane sorbet . . . for this one (*A putti*) just a cup of coffee. You see – I'm not that cheap. You look terrible.
(KRACKLITE *has looked away, affected by the talk of food.*)

KRACKLITE: I'm not hungry.

FLAVIA: You can watch me eat. This is an expensive camera.

(*She hands it back to him.*)

KRACKLITE: It's a birthday present.

FLAVIA: Who gave it to you?

KRACKLITE: I gave it to myself.

FLAVIA: Caspasian always said you were a generous man.

KRACKLITE: (*With sadness and anger*) He would know.

There is a silence. KRACKLITE looks very flushed, hot, sad and uncomfortable. He bows his head. She takes photos of him – with his camera. He wearily puts his hand up over his face.

FLAVIA: (*Sympathetically*) You look like a tired old man who's just come up out of the sea.

KRACKLITE. (*Sheepishly*) I've *tried* a little drowning.

FLAVIA: Let's try a little more. (*Takes the film from his camera.*) Come to my studio. I'll process your film while you take a shower and we'll see which comes out of the bath the more developed.

FLAVIA guides KRACKLITE to her sports car parked nearby. They get in and drive off – leaving the Piazza Fountains splashing in the early-morning light.

Section Twenty-seven: Afternoon, Monday, 20 January 1986

SCENE 45: FLAVIA'S STUDIO WITH KRACKLITE

Flavia's studio. An elegant room – modern. Built in the last ten years. Generous proportions. Fourth-storey apartment. Photographic equipment. Drying cupboards, developing tanks, enlarger, etc. Lots of photographs. A large black and red-corded couch. KRACKLITE and FLAVIA – their hair wet from the shower – sit in white dressing-gowns on the couch. They are flicking through black-and-white photographic albums of Flavia's work. For the most part the photos are of statuary, buildings and paintings. There is a high proportion of statuary associated with water – Tritons, water deities and fountains. FLAVIA gets up and puts on a gramophone record.

FLAVIA: Io says that there are twenty thousand life-sized statues in Rome – the population of the Vatican on a Sunday. At the time of Augustus there were twice that number – mostly of him. Rome is full of male statues – most of them nude and most of them associated with water – (*Provoking*) fifteen thousand, wet, male nudes – what do you think that means?

KRACKLITE: (*Dismissively*) It's hot in summer.

FLAVIA: I'll show you someone who I always thought looked like you.

(*She flips through photos of water gods, etc. – and comes up with the portrait of Andrea Doria.*)

KRACKLITE: (*Reads on the back:*) Andrea Doria as Neptune by Bronzino.

FLAVIA: Stand up . . . over there. (*Compares* KRACKLITE *to the photo – she props it up on a stand.*) Let me take a photo of you as Andrea Doria. Hold this! (*Gives him a curtain rod to hold as a trident.*) Just a minute.

(*She gets out a tripod, camera, lights – very adroitly and swiftly –* KRACKLITE *acquiesces and removes his dressing-gown – looking rather dazed and tired.*)

KRACKLITE: No – I don't think I want to do it.

FLAVIA: Yes, you do – look over there.

FLAVIA adjusts the lights to correspond with the painting's lighting. KRACKLITE shifts about uneasily. She comes over to him and arranges the towel. She takes various photos – adjusting the lights and lenses. Then she stops, stretches and watches him. He is standing very still.

FLAVIA: All right – you can relax now.

She adroitly takes the film out of the camera, enters a cupboard room where she switches on a red photographic light – and busies herself with developing the film.

KRACKLITE puts his borrowed dressing-gown back on. He wanders about the room, turning over folders of photographs of fountain figures, statues. He wanders into a small anteroom – dimly in the semi-darkness he sees rows and rows of photographs pinned up on the wall. He raises the slats of the room's Venetian blinds to see better. He goes closer. What he sees gives him a shock.

KRACKLITE looks at rows and rows of photographs of himself and, parallel underneath, rows and rows of photos of LOUISA. FLAVIA has been taking photos of them both since the very first day they were in Rome at the Pantheon restaurant. Many of the situations presented in the photos we recognize – but many we don't – KRACKLITE and we, the audience, now realize what FLAVIA has been doing. There are shots of KRACKLITE eating, stuffing himself at the Pantheon, at the Exhibition inauguration, of KRACKLITE vomiting, of him throwing food away at the Baths of Villa Adriana, of him shouting at CASPASIAN, of him arguing with the other members of the Committee, of him looking tired, ill, and exhausted. Underneath, the parallel photos of LOUISA show her eating, stuffing her mouth with cake, laughing, holding hands with CASPASIAN, kissing CASPASIAN, eating with CASPASIAN, shopping, going to the cinema and the theatre with CASPASIAN. At the end of each row there is an ominous space – obviously there are more photos to come. KRACKLITE stares aghast. He weeps to see the deterioration of his marriage set before him in pictures.

Very quietly FLAVIA has come into the room behind him. She watches him. Gently – she approaches him and touches him. He should be furious – but he isn't. He's too appalled at the visual evidence to feel anger at the way FLAVIA has behaved as a *voyeur*. They look at one another – then FLAVIA smiles and kisses him. She opens her robe and hugs him. She takes off her robe. She is beautiful, her skin is very white – and her body is very symmetrical – all orbs and cylinders. She elegantly and provocatively closes the Venetian blind to let the photos fade back into the orange shadow. The music slowly fades to hear the canvas blind gently tapping on the sill in a draught. FLAVIA takes KRACKLITE by the hand and leads him . . .

. . . back to the couch where the camera on its tripod is still set up. She motions him to sit down. He watches her. She has a much maturer body than LOUISA. He steps forwards and cups his hand over her belly. He kisses her and then they make love. Behind them, a still life of photographic magazines suddenly rustles in a draught – it's not certain for a moment what caused it. There is the sound of a distant door shutting – it doesn't disturb the lovers. Suddenly CASPASIAN is standing there with keys dangling in his hand. Without undue stealth, he moves to the camera and, holding the cable release, he takes a flash photo.

KRACKLITE – humiliated – is caught in the flash.
With the horrible realization that he has possibly been the victim of a set-up job, possibly even to help complete the set of photos of his humiliation pinned on the wall of the adjacent room, KRACKLITE freezes. He makes no movement to get himself out of the embarrassing circumstances – it seems another inevitable part of his humiliating illness. CASPASIAN crosses the room and switches off the record-player. Slowly KRACKLITE disentangles himself from FLAVIA. CASPASIAN stands in the light where KRACKLITE himself stood for FLAVIA as Andrea Doria.

CASPASIAN: So . . . what do you have to say for yourself, Signor Kracklite – making love in the afternoon to my sister?

FLAVIA: (*Angrily warning him*) Caspasian!

CASPASIAN sits down on the couch beside his sister, who begins to brush her hair with a scarlet comb. KRACKLITE, sitting upright on the couch, watches them both. Strangely, in the circumstances, he looks dignified. They make a surreal, suggestive trio. CASPASIAN, neat, meticulous, smiling: the naked and beautiful FLAVIA, combing her hair – her face expressionless; KRACKLITE, large, pale, vulnerable, with his uncombed hair awry. We have seen three people sit on a sofa once before – at the Inauguration of the Exhibition – with KRACKLITE now sitting in for the senile BATTISTINO.

KRACKLITE: (*Slowly – and with difficulty keeping his temper – and also a little pompously because of it*) I'd say that you and my wife are entirely oblivious as to the time or the place of your love-making.

He covers his nakedness with the discarded dressing-gown – he looks like Andrea Doria sitting down.

CASPASIAN: Well – you have now made it plain – so to speak – that what is good for the goose – is good for the philanderer. (*With a smile*) An English proverb?

KRACKLITE: (*Furiously*) Philanderer?!

CASPASIAN: Your wife is very beautiful . . . Signor Kracklite . . . especially when she is pregnant . . .

KRACKLITE: She may be pregnant, Speckler – but not with your child.

CASPASIAN: True . . . I have *you* to be grateful for that. Your child – shall we say – is the most perfect contraceptive.

(KRACKLITE *leaps up, furious. He hurls himself at* CASPASIAN.)

KRACKLITE: You bastard!

KRACKLITE and CASPASIAN topple over on to the thick-pile carpet. They struggle. KRACKLITE's weight is a match for CASPASIAN's strength. KRACKLITE starts to pant and then groan. His stomach pains double him up. CASPASIAN crawls free and stands up. KRACKLITE is sprawled – humiliated – on the floor. CASPASIAN meticulously brushes down his crumpled suit . . .

FLAVIA: (*To* CASPASIAN) There now – does that make you satisfied?

FLAVIA gets up from the couch and puts on her dressing-gown. She and then CASPASIAN help KRACKLITE on to the couch.

FLAVIA: (*As though to a child*) Architects must be careful.

CASPASIAN: So must cuckolds.

Despite his pain, KRACKLITE takes a wild swing at CASPASIAN – and lands him a punch on the nose. It bleeds. CASPASIAN is about to retaliate, but FLAVIA holds him back.

FLAVIA: Kracklite – sick men must be careful.

FLAVIA hands KRACKLITE a drink – CASPASIAN dabs his nose with a spotlessly clean handkerchief . . . it doesn't stop bleeding, so he leaves the room for the bathroom. FLAVIA opens the Venetian blinds.

FLAVIA: (*Shouting to* CASPASIAN) Don't get your blood on my white towels. (*To* KRACKLITE) I'll call you a taxi.

KRACKLITE nods. FLAVIA brings KRACKLITE'S clothes through from an outside room. KRACKLITE dresses beside the Andrea Doria portrait. Anger, frustration, humiliation are written on his face. The lights from the Venetian blinds stripe his body diagonally. CASPASIAN re-enters the room – still dabbing his nose. There is blood on his shirt and jacket which irritates him – he spends more effort attempting to get the blood off the jacket than stopping it flowing from his nose.

CASPASIAN: (*With some pique*) I take it that you will now give Louisa as much freedom as you've taken for yourself?

KRACKLITE: It's too late for giving anything that's already been taken.

CASPASIAN: None the less, I'm sure you'd not want her to know . . . ?

FLAVIA takes the rolls of negative out of the drying cupboard. She holds the negative (the Piazza Navona photos) up to the light from the window.

FLAVIA: There are enough stomachs here, Kracklite, to have several illnesses.

(*She puts them in a transparent envelope.*)

KRACKLITE: (*Putting on his jacket*) And the one in the camera?

(*There is a momentary silence. He takes the proffered negatives from* FLAVIA.)

Well?

(*He holds out his hand for the film from the camera.*)

CASPASIAN (*Sarcastically*) So how is the Exhibition progressing, Kracklite? Are you fully in control – would you say?

KRACKLITE: What's that supposed to mean?

CASPASIAN: If you don't feel in control of things, Kracklite, you couldn't do better than to hand over the reins to someone else.

KRACKLITE: That person being yourself? Is this blackmail? . . . Do you think that preventing my wife from knowing that I was screwing your sister is worth giving you control of the Boullée Exhibition, for Christ's sake?

FLAVIA: (*Smiling*) Thank you, Stourley, for the compliment – but don't worry – Caspasian is always over-reaching himself. If you wanted a really serious quarrel, I'm sorry – but – there was no film in the camera.

The camera in question is fixed on the tripod where FLAVIA left it. She throws a catch on the back of the camera – the camera back swings open to show that indeed there is no film there. She depresses the flash several times to show how it was possible to flash without taking a picture. KRACKLITE, dressed, leaves the room.

CASPASIAN and FLAVIA go to the window and lift the Venetian blind, revealing a view of the EUR building outside . . . the Mussolini building the Romans call 'the square Colosseum'. It's the last in the succession of Roman buildings associated with

Boullée – this time it's a building that – possibly – could have been influenced by Boullée.

Time-lapse 8
It's late afternoon – the sky is reddening. KRACKLITE – down in the forecourt – gets into his taxi – the taxi leaves – and imperceptibly exaggerated time takes over. Accompanied by the eighth and last of the grandiloquent 'Roman architectural music' pieces, the afternoon sky deepens in colour, the shadows lengthen, night falls, the artificial lights of distant Rome come on. The moon rises.

Section Twenty-eight: Noon, Saturday, 25 January 1986

SCENE 46: FORO ITALICO
At the Foro Italico stadium FREDERICO and CASPASIAN are making preparations to restore some of the damage done to the statues and masonry. They are accompanied by six workmen in newspaper hats and overalls. Two of the statues have been wrapped in see-through plastic sheets, a third is surrounded by scaffolding and protective netting. There are wheelbarrows, ladders, hoses, paint-remover, theodolites, architect's equipment, cement-mixers, piles of gravel and sand, kerbstones, facing stones and numerous tools. The area has been cordoned off.
In the foreground is a wooden trestle table, on which are a selection of stone-sculpted fingers, toes, genitals and an arm and a leg – items of restoration which CASPASIAN and FREDERICO aim to replace on the statues. CASPASIAN is his usual elegant self. FREDERICO rides up on his motorbike, coming fast around the curve of the stadium. CASPASIAN greets him, pulls him aside and speaks to him.

CASPASIAN: Kracklite's finished. He looks a mess. He's grotesque. (*Insultingly mimes* KRACKLITE's *bulk, his belly, his walk.*) Trettorio says he won't last till August . . . I've found another 16 million from the publicity account – the catalogue's never going to be finished anyway – Kracklite wanted it all in colour. (*Mimics him in a broad jokey American accent, stretching*

out the syllables.) 'Now *my* architect Boullée knew more about colour than Leonardo da Vinci . . .'
FREDERICO: '. . . and more about publicity than Michelangelo Buonarroti . . .'
CASPASIAN: '. . . more about making love than Casanova.'
FREDERICO: (*With both of them laughing*) What does his wife say about that?
CASPASIAN: (*Airily and tapping his nose*) She's non-committal . . . but she's said enough to know that big men don't necessarily have big cocks. And (*Laughing*) from what I've seen of Kracklite – she's right.
(*They laugh loudly.*)

Section Twenty-nine: Late Afternoon, Thursday, 30 January 1986

SCENE 47: BOOKSHOP
It's raining. It's getting dark. KRACKLITE is wandering in a large bookstore. He is wearing a large raincoat for the purpose of deliberately stealing books.
He is flicking through the art books. He finds a coloured reproduction of Bronzino's *Andrea Doria*. He looks over his shoulder to see if anyone is looking. There are several customers and one or two assistants in the store. They are taking no notice of him. With his finger lodged in the page, KRACKLITE picks up the book and wanders on. He selects a solid-looking hard-cover book – oversize – Vesalius' *Anatomy* – identified by the 'exploded' anatomical drawing on the cover. KRACKLITE slyly rips out the *Andrea Doria* portrait from the first book and puts the torn page into the Vesalius. He then – after a cursory look around – puts the Vesalius into the front of his bulky raincoat. An assistant is watching him.
KRACKLITE browses the photographic books section – prominent on display are several copies of Flavia's book – featuring a male nude on the front cover. Each copy is wrapped in Cellophane – so KRACKLITE can't open the pages – he looks at the price tag – it's expensive. He raises his eyebrows and blows through his teeth in

an exaggerated way. It's a show put on for the assistant who is now openly watching him.
KRACKLITE makes his way to the door of the shop – on the way out he selects several coloured postcards from a rack. He quite openly puts them in his pocket and makes for the door – it's obvious that he expects to be stopped. He dodges the assistant and runs out into the street.
The assistant chases him along the street for 40-odd yards. He is in his shirt-sleeves and it's pouring with rain. KRACKLITE – puffing and already exhausted – hails a taxi, gets in and drives off. The assistant runs after the taxi and thumps on the back window. KRACKLITE thumbs his nose at him through the window. The assistant stands with his hair plastered down to his head by the downpour of rain.
The taxi passes a butcher's shop well stocked with red meat. KRACKLITE looks curiously, and then – opening the Vesalius – looks at the portrait of Doria. The portrait and the 'exploded' view of the stomach are laid open side by side in the book.

Section Thirty: Noon, Friday, 31st January 1986

SCENE 48: FLAVIA'S STUDIO WITH LOUISA
In Flavia's photographic studio/flat. The same furniture – the same couch – as when Kracklite had his photos taken. LOUISA – naked, very noticeably pregnant, and feeling self-conscious and nervous, is having her photos taken. She's standing in front of the red-corded, black couch. While talking, FLAVIA is constantly taking pictures.

FLAVIA: Hold your head up a little . . . why did you come in the end? Caspasian said you were reluctant.

LOUISA: He convinced me – he said you were very good . . . and wanted a child yourself.

FLAVIA: (*With a smile*) Did he indeed? Do you really think that's why I asked to photograph you . . .? Sit down, can you, and take off your shoes . . . and put them on the couch.

LOUISA: (*Nervously*) What does that mean?

FLAVIA: It means that you take your shoes off and put them on the couch! How long have you got to go?
LOUISA: A month. It's due on the 15th of February.
FLAVIA: The Exhibition will be started by then. Sit more to the side. Are you going back to Chicago?
LOUISA: We'll see – it depends . . .
FLAVIA: On what?
LOUISA: On . . . on Kracklite . . . his health . . . other things . . .
FLAVIA: Stretch your legs a little. He was here last week . . . can you kneel up a little . . .
LOUISA: That's uncomfortable . . . and too revealing . . .
FLAVIA: It looks rather beautiful to me . . . (*A little sarcastically*) It's a bit difficult now to hide the fact that you're pregnant.
LOUISA: (*Half-nervous laugh*) That's not what I meant.
FLAVIA: Put your hands back on your lap then. (*Pause.*) Of all the female statues in Rome, not one of them is pregnant – I've searched – don't you think that's strange –
LOUISA: (*Interrupting*) Who was here last week?
FLAVIA: Kracklite. (*Looking up significantly from the viewfinder*) Having his photo taken . . . there's some prints on the table.
(*She indicates a small table beside the couch –* LOUISA *stretches up to look.*) Have a look.
LOUISA: (*Doing as* FLAVIA *says – she picks up a photo of Kracklite as Andrea Doria*) Why's he standing like that?
FLAVIA: (*With a laugh*) He's posing as the Old Man of the Sea (*She continues to take photos.*)
LOUISA: Was that his idea?
FLAVIA: No – mine. Don't you think that's a good pose for him?
LOUISA: (*With a contemptuous smile*) . . . and *pose* is the word!
FLAVIA: Dear old Kracklite – dressed – or undressed – as Andrea Doria.
LOUISA: Was he an architect too?
FLAVIA: (*Laughing*) No – at least I don't think so – not all fat, middle-aged gentlemen build buildings you know. Not that

Kracklite builds buildings – (*Suddenly angry*) he makes monuments – just like that old fart Boullée . . . in fact Kracklite is a bit of a monument himself, isn't he? . . . and there are enough monuments around here.

LOUISA: Why on earth do you suppose he feels so at home here? Nobody has to live in the Tomb of Augustus . . .

FLAVIA: . . . or the Pantheon . . .

LOUISA: . . . or the Colosseum . . .

FLAVIA: . . . or Trajan's Column . . .

LOUISA: . . . or St Peter's . . .

FLAVIA: . . . or *that* Mussolini building out there (*Points to the window*) . . . it's all show and bluster and bits of masonry.

LOUISA: (*Laughing*) Kracklite's really got into you – hasn't he?

FLAVIA: (*Laughing with her*) Hold it there.

(LOUISA *is three-quarters back-turned to the camera – she holds the large photo of Kracklite in her left hand – she is half in and half out of the light.*)

Why don't you take up the same position?

LOUISA: (*With a laugh*) What – posing as the Old Woman of the Sea – next to the Old Man of the Sea?

FLAVIA: (*Laughing*) Neptune had a young wife.

LOUISA: I can see that you think we're inseparable (*implying that she means just the opposite*).

FLAVIA: (*With a smile*) Aren't you? (*Clicks – and with a laugh*) Though it's difficult, I admit, to see who is the more expectant!

(*They both laugh – loudly.*)

LOUISA: You were right that night outside the Pantheon – seven years was too long.

(*They continue to laugh.*)

Section Thirty-one: Afternoon, Friday, 31 January 1986

SCENE 49: VITTORIANO MAIN HALL: EXPULSION OF KRACKLITE

In the exhibition gallery, the exhibition is taking shape – large models of several of Boullée's buildings are in place – an electrician is testing the lights on the interior of the Newton

Memorial Sphere – switching through a system of daylight, moonlight, dusk and dawn. Four carpenters are hoisting up giant, blow-up black-and-white photographs of buildings in Rome – inspirational buildings to Boullée – buildings that we have already seen – and photographed from exactly the same angle as we have seen them –

1. The Augustan Mausoleum
2. The Pantheon
3. The Colosseum
4. The Baths of Villa Adriana
5. St Peter's Square
6. The Forum
7. Piazza Navona
8. The EUR Building

Several reproduction blow-ups of Piranesi engravings are lying discarded.
To one side – and partly in the shadow – KRACKLITE is feeding a movable photocopying machine with the Andrea Doria reproduction – turning out twenty or more copies – he is watching fascinated as the 'bellies' churn out of the photocopier . . . FREDERICO and JULIO enter and see KRACKLITE.

JULIO: Kracklite – we've got to see you!

FREDERICO: The bank's stopped the cashflow.

JULIO: Caspetti is complaining that the Exhibition isn't Roman enough.

KRACKLITE: That's absurd!

FREDERICO: Is it? You've forbidden the Piranesi blow-up photographs.

KRACKLITE: That's not true! It was Caspasian's idea – to save money!

JULIO: Well – Caspetti has to be pacified. Stourley – I'm sorry, but it looks as though Trettorio has mentioned to him that you are a sick man . . .

FREDERICO: . . . he wants you to have a medical examination!

KRACKLITE: (*Furiously*) I'm not a sick man! And I've just had one!

JULIO: Caspetti has asked that Caspasian should be made director of the Exhibition . . .

KRACKLITE: He what!?

FREDERICO: He thinks that the Exhibition is too gloomy – too melodramatic.

KRACKLITE: He hasn't seen the lighting!

FREDERICO: (*With a grin*) He thinks that you've got too many domestic problems on your mind.

KRACKLITE: He what! What's that to do with him! He's throwing in every excuse he can think of.

JULIO: He thinks that Caspasian will give the Exhibition a more optimistic and . . . Roman bias.

KRACKLITE: Over my dead body!

FREDERICO: Not a bad prognosis.

KRACKLITE: (*Advancing threateningly in* FREDERICO's *direction*) What was that? I'm as fit as you are.

JULIO: Stourley – you know that's not true!

FREDERICO: Are you going to punch me on the nose again?

KRACKLITE: Caspetti was against Boullée from the start . . . he said he reminded him of Hell. I'll give him Hell!

IO: (*Walking across the room and joining the trio*) Look, Kracklite – I'm afraid they've put up an ultimatum. You'll have to resign if you want the Exhibition to go on. We can't let it collapse now. How was the medical?

KRACKLITE: You're damn right we can't! (*Quietly*) I have to go back for the results.

IO: Let Caspetti believe Caspasian is in charge.

KRACKLITE: No, I can't!

IO: Stourley – I don't think we have a choice.

KRACKLITE: I'll think of something.

IO: Don't be absurd. We open in twelve days.

KRACKLITE: I'll find the money. How much do we need?

IO: Battistino says 30 million lire.

KRACKLITE: I thought Battistino was dead – I saw him at the hospital.

FREDERICO: What hospital?

JULIO: He was raising funds.

KRACKLITE: Raising funds . . .? How can a dead man raise funds?

JULIO: Insurance.

FREDERICO: They don't call him Lazarus for nothing.
KRACKLITE: If a dead man can raise funds – what can a sick man do? I can raise funds.
FREDERICO: You need Caspasian to handle it.
KRACKLITE: And where the hell is Caspasian? (*Working himself up into a fury*) He's the one that's been spending all the money! He's been behind this all along! (*Facing* IO) That bastard son of yours was determined to get his hands on this Exhibition from the start. (*White with fury*) Where is he?
IO: (*Trying to cool and restrain* KRACKLITE *– but not without some embarrassment to himself on account of his son*) Stourley – he's not here – he's out.
KRACKLITE: Out where?
FREDERICO: Raising funds.
KRACKLITE: I bet he's not out raising funds for Boullée!
FREDERICO: (*Provocatively*) You're right!
KRACKLITE: Oh? – then what for?
FREDERICO: (*Quietly*) Some restoration work.
KRACKLITE: Where? . . . and doing what?
FREDERICO: Restoring Mussolini's Foro Italico.
KRACKLITE: So that's where all the money's been going! *I*'ve been subsidizing that fascist playground!
IO: You can't say that, Kracklite.
FREDERICO: And you certainly couldn't prove it! (*With pointed sarcasm*) Anyway, don't you think Boullée would have been the first to applaud such a *visionary* piece of architectural theatre? (*He slow hand-claps in ironic reference to the night they clapped at the Pantheon.*)
KRACKLITE: (*A little sheepishly*) Why isn't Caspasian raising funds for this? (*Waving his arm over the Exhibition.*) And look – look – (*With rising anger*) if they can do it with Battistino – they can do it with me . . . at least I'm not faking!
FREDERICO: (*Pitilessly*) So you admit you're ill!
KRACKLITE: (*Furiously*) Ill – hell – I'm a walking medical case! (*Desperately*) But I'm still fit enough to tackle Caspetti and Caspasian and all of you! – I'll find that money even if I have to steal it!
IO: (*Compassionately*) Stourley!

KRACKLITE bundles into his raincoat and strides off across the hall – papers flying in his wake . . . he comes back and snatches up his photocopies of Andrea Doria and hurries out again. The others watch him in disbelief . . . and some scorn.

Section Thirty-two: Late Evening, Friday, 31 January 1986

SCENE 50: THE KRACKLITE APARTMENT; LOUISA LEAVES

KRACKLITE is standing on the bed in his apartment bedroom – the room is in a mess. He has the whole collection of his photocopies spread out on the floor – the Augustus stomachs, the Boullée stomachs, the stomachs of the statues he photographed in the Piazza Navona, the Andrea Doria stomachs . . . and the photographs of his own stomach taken by FLAVIA – there are some thirty-odd images – all of them marked by Kracklite. He is drinking whisky, he slumps to a sitting position on the bed. He has propped a mirror up against the furniture and, with his shirt undone, he is comparing his stomach with the photographs. LOUISA comes in and makes him jump. She carries a photographic folder which she dumps on the bed with her handbag.

KRACKLITE: Where the hell have you been?

LOUISA: (*Airily*) Well, wouldn't you like to know? But it's all right, Kracklite – we'll keep it in the family.

KRACKLITE: What's that supposed to mean?

LOUISA: It means, Stourley – that you can have no complaint about me that I can't about you. It seems we go to the same doctor and the same photographer . . .? But not with the same complaint, eh, Kracklite? Though – who knows? – your belly's about as big as mine!

LOUISA goes to the wardrobe and takes out a half-packed suitcase. She begins to take dresses off hangers and pack them. The rest of the dialogue is conducted with her packing – breaking off now and again to argue or make a point. KRACKLITE watches her all the time. When necessary, to get to the other side of the room, she treads between Kracklite's photographs on the floor –

peremptorily brushing KRACKLITE's face with the hem of her skirt.

KRACKLITE: (*Exasperated*) I've made some decisions.

LOUISA: Oh!

KRACKLITE: I'm going to mortgage the house in Chicago.

LOUISA: Oh yes – what for – it's my house – don't you remember – you built it for me . . . with all its draughty wide open spaces and its rounded corners where you can't fit any furniture . . . and its . . .

KRACKLITE: (*Interrupting*) And I'm changing the beneficiaries of the trust fund.

LOUISA: Oh no, you don't.

KRACKLITE: I need two hundred thousand dollars fast.

LOUISA: Caspasian could get that sort of money by snapping his fingers.

KRACKLITE: Snapping his fingers! I could snap his neck. He's snapped you up . . . He's not snapping up my exhibition . . . and I am changing my will.

LOUISA: (*Contemptuously*) What will, for God's sake?

KRACKLITE: I am not letting this exhibition slip through my fingers if it's the last thing I do.

LOUISA: It will be – the way that you're carrying on. And you're not going to prejudice *my* child's future for the sake of another unfinished Kracklite fiasco.

KRACKLITE: *Our* child . . . *our* child, or have you forgotten who the father is? *And* he is going to be born in America!

LOUISA: Is he?

KRACKLITE: As soon as this exhibition is open, you and I are going back home.

LOUISA: Oh really? (*Provocatively*) I quite like the idea of him being born in Italy. (*Sarcastically*) I might call him Luigi.

KRACKLITE: (*Very sourly*) I was sure you were going to call him Caspasian. How do you know it'll be a boy?

LOUISA: By the shape of my stomach.

KRACKLITE: God! Who told you that? Our medical architect Caspasian Speckler?

LOUISA: (*Airily*) As a matter of fact – his sister.

KRACKLITE: God! Have they all taken courses in gynaecology?

LOUISA: It seems to me that *you* have a suspiciously

obsessional interest in stomachs . . . masculine stomachs . . . you're not going off women are you, Kracklite? If you are – here's something to remind you of what they look like.

She adroitly places the photographs that FLAVIA took of her in a line at the bottom of the ones already on the floor – till all the photos on the floor look like a giant game of solo patience. KRACKLITE is too surprised by the photos to react. LOUISA slams into the bathroom. She turns the bathtaps full on. KRACKLITE – sprawled on the floor – looks at the photos – they are suggestively erotic. He fingers them. Picks them up, fascinated and appalled. The large mirror propped at the foot of the bed catches his reflection. He gets up, visibly shaken. He walks to the bathroom door.

KRACKLITE: This is appalling – they're obscene!

LOUISA: (*Through the door and the noise of the taps*) Are they?

KRACKLITE: Exhibiting yourself like this!

LOUISA: It's for Art, Kracklite – (*With derisory sarcasm*) everything's permissible for Art. I mean, look at our marriage. Art first, Kracklite second, the rest a long way down the line.

KRACKLITE: It's my child in there!

LOUISA: (*Laughs loudly.*) *Your* child . . . what do you feel, Kracklite? – do you feel prostituted? (LOUISA *comes out of the bathroom carrying clothes.*) I'm moving out.

KRACKLITE: Where are you going?

LOUISA: If it's still any of your business – which I doubt – I'm going to stay with Caspasian. He'll take care of me until after the baby is born. After that I don't know.

KRACKLITE: Please don't leave me now. Please.

LOUISA: It's too late for that now, Stourley. Besides . . . I'm due in a month – the Exhibition opens in twelve days . . . and you're unreliable – I have no intention of losing this child – or of dropping it too soon. Let's face it, Stourley – I just don't need you any more . . .

LOUISA leaves the room. KRACKLITE is slouched against the outside of the bathroom door, staring towards the open window that looks out over the Mausoleum of Augustus.

Section Thirty-three: Afternoon, Monday, 10 February 1986

SCENE 51: DRIVE WITH VESALIUS

KRACKLITE is sitting in the front passenger seat of IO's car. They are driving through a sunlit Rome – a part of the city rich in Renaissance and post-Renaissance buildings.

On KRACKLITE's lap is a heavy book – a hard-cover copy of Vesalius' *Anatomy* – the one he stole from the bookshop. It is opened at a plate showing a half-stripped-down male corpse with the various organs and features of the stomach much in evidence. With a deliberation it takes us a minute or two to comprehend, KRACKLITE is wedging a corner of the hard-bound book into his stomach. The opposing corner of the book is wedged in the passenger's glove compartment. KRACKLITE experimentally and repeatedly throws his weight against the book corner. IO has noticed but says nothing. They drive silently. IO looks for a suitable moment to speak.

IO: (*Making one accusation to cover a more sensitive one*) Stourley? Can I speak frankly?

KRACKLITE: You normally do.

IO: I hardly mention it, but it's been noticed – (*Hesitates*) – that you steal postcards.

KRACKLITE: (*With a bitter laugh*) Has it? It can't be as heinous as stealing an exhibition. Postcards are part of a city's publicity campaign – I am just redistributing the adverts.

(IO *smiles – they drive in silence for a few moments.*)

IO: Look, Stourley – we want to see you well again . . . and the Exhibition can now look after itself. Whatever the results of the medical examination – everyone feels that you can do no more for Boullée – he's in safe hands – why not take a well-deserved rest? Don't worry. Boullée will be celebrated in the way that he should . . . We would like you to open the Exhibition – as you should – and then you must leave the running of the Exhibition to us . . . after the opening – why don't you go back to Chicago and take a well-deserved rest . . .?

(*They pull up outside the hospital.*)

Shall I wait for you?
KRACKLITE: No – it's all right.
IO: You know that you can get that book in paperback now?
KRACKLITE: Yes, I know . . . I just like hard covers.

Section Thirty-four: Afternoon, Monday, 10 February 1986

SCENE 52: HOSPITAL CLOISTER
KRACKLITE is at the hospital. A wide corridor/reception area has numerous Roman artefacts exhibited along its length. The corridor is open to a sunlit courtyard. Occasionally an intercom call for a waiting patient echoes along the corridor.
There is the sound of birds – sparrows – and occasionally a distant aircraft. There is a small fountain running into a basin. KRACKLITE is writing a postcard of the Pantheon as he waits to be called.

Monday 10 February '86

Dear Etienne-Louis,
It's no good, Etienne. I'm ousted – kicked out of the exhibition I spent the last ten years of my life planning. It's Caspasian's fault. He's run off with my wife, my child and our exhibition . . . but I've an idea. Supposing you came to open the exhibition. Why don't you come? How about that? That would show them . . .

The intercom calls KRACKLITE's name. He looks up and then continues writing:

You could stay in my apartment. Louisa's not there any more. I don't sleep too well – but I'm sure we'd manage . . .

The intercom calls his name a second time. He finishes writing:

Yours,
Stourley Kracklite
(Architect)

KRACKLITE gets up, walks over to a postbox and posts his card. He then walks forward to greet DOCTOR AMANSA who has been quietly waiting for him to finish writing the postcard.
KRACKLITE and AMANSA walk down the hospital gallery – a wide corridor with high ceilings and a stone floor. All along one side of the corridor is a line of Roman busts on plinths or pedestals. Hospital staff occasionally walk by. The DOCTOR and KRACKLITE slowly walk down the corridor's length. He draws KRACKLITE's attention to the portrait busts.

AMANSA: (*Coming to the first bust*) Galba . . . a miserable sort of man . . . bisexual . . . fancied mature slaves, especially if they had been a little mutilated . . . all his freed men had no fingers on the left hands . . . he's dead – died screaming . . . in a cellar. (*They walk on. They stop again.*)
Titus . . . he started well . . . soon became greedy . . . disembowelled on the Tiber steps . . . he's dead, died screaming . . .(*They walk on.*)
Hadrian . . . as you know, an architect of note . . . put a lot of faith in stones . . . died peacefully . . . planning a Temple to Wisdom . . . still . . . (*Shrugs*) . . . he's dead . . . Nero – best not to talk about him – burnt Rome, caused untold misery – deserved to die; died screaming in a summerhouse.
(*They come to an unnamed bust and the* DOCTOR *stops.*)
Unknown . . . no name . . . he looks serene enough, let's suppose he was you . . . same fleshy face . . . what happened to him? How did he die?

KRACKLITE: He died at noon in a parked car in a Chicago precinct with the stockmarket news on the car radio – he had shaved off his beard . . . he was wearing an English suit . . . (*Looking at his feet*) and Italian shoes . . .

AMANSA: (*Quietly*) Is that what you want?

KRACKLITE: No . . . he died later – aged seventy-one, the same age as Boullée . . . sitting in a garden at four o'clock in the afternoon – facing south somewhere near Rome . . . near the sound of water. His six-year-old grandson playing on the gravel . . . his wife – (*With feeling and a touch of regret*) his *second* wife . . . picking the orange blossom.

AMANSA: A little sentimental?
KRACKLITE: (*Shrugging and smiling*) What of it? When you're seventy-one you can afford a little sentiment.
AMANSA: (*Gently*) Far from home?
KRACKLITE: That should be no particular worry.
AMANSA: (*Quietly*) A sort of late-spring death?
KRACKLITE: Late spring?
(*A long pause as the import of the conversation sinks in.*)
How far into late spring?
AMANSA: Maybe the last week of May . . . the first week of June . . .?
KRACKLITE: June . . .? (*Lingeringly considers the warm month of June.*) June? (*Says it a second time – making an unspoken calculation – then, with a smile*) Do you do this with all your patients?
AMANSA: (*Sympathetically*) I admit it's not the first time . . . though the details might not in another case be so 'architectural' . . . (*Smiles.*) There is some comfort to be had in contemplating the folly of so many dead . . . don't you think? . . . and more comfort still in contemplating the continuity . . .?

They look along the line of busts – alternately caught in and out of the sunlight. KRACKLITE goes back along the line and strokes, caresses or touches each bust. He stops at Hadrian. He puts his hand on its head.

Section Thirty-five: Evening, Tuesday, 11 February 1986

SCENE 53: VITTORIANO COLONNADE

Up on the colonnade parapet – CASPASIAN, FREDERICO and IO, FLAVIA, CLAUDIA, MORI, three officials and four electricians are arranging the green laser beams. They flash out over Rome in the direction of the Pantheon, the Piazza del Popolo, the Augusteum, the Piazza Navona and St Peter's. As they turn each one on, there is a cry of surprise, delight and excitement. LOUISA – looking very pregnant – is there with CASPASIAN. She looks happy and relaxed.

Section Thirty-six: Evening, Tuesday, 11 February 1986

SCENE 54: OUTDOOR CAFÉ/BAR NEAR VITTORIANO

It's evening. Nine o'clock. At a table in a restaurant open to the street KRACKLITE is seated, drinking. He is surrounded by his books and papers. There are other diners, and the location permits excellent views of the Victor Emanuel, the Piazza de Venezia and the Campidoglio. The eight-year-old BOY and his MOTHER – both smartly dressed for public dining – come and sit down at a nearby table. KRACKLITE is drunk. He is maudlin, belligerent, reckless and sentimental.

KRACKLITE: (*Speaking to the* BOY) Hello. Your mother is very beautiful this evening.

MOTHER and SON look at KRACKLITE and both smile. They do indeed both look radiant.

KRACKLITE, part courteous gesture, part sexist gallantry, part true response to their exceptional beauty –

KRACKLITE: What makes you both so beautiful?

The BOY'S MOTHER asks her son for a translation. The BOY translates for her. With a sensuous smile, she makes a reply in Italian.

BOY: My mother says that we sleep too much. (*Adds his own comment.*) My father has left us to sleep a lot.

KRACKLITE: That was bad of him.

BOY: (*A little put out*) If it makes us look beautiful, why was it bad of him?

KRACKLITE: (*To the* WOMAN) Has he left you for good?

BOY: Oh no . . . he's waiting for us.

KRACKLITE: In the residence?

(*He points at the apartment block.*)

BOY: (*Laughing*) No. In Ventimiglia.

KRACKLITE: (*Surprised*) In Ventimiglia?

(*He mockingly accentuates the syllables – exactly like the loudspeaker voice on the station at the start of the film.*)

BOY: (*Frankly*) Yes. In the cemetery at Ventimiglia.

KRACKLITE: What's he waiting there for?

KRACKLITE realizes the import and stops. He looks at the BOY who stares back for a long moment. KRACKLITE's mood rapidly changes. He is caught off-guard, he thinks deliberately.

KRACKLITE: (*Angrily*) That's not fair! What are you trying to do?

He rises out of his chair – books and papers fall to the floor. He walks unsteadily around to their table. He waves his finger in front of the BOY's nose.

KRACKLITE: Are you trying to tell me something?

He grabs the BOY by the shirt front – his MOTHER begins to shout at KRACKLITE – in Italian.

KRACKLITE: What makes you think I care what happened to your father?

The BOY looks at him and then at his MOTHER, and then back at KRACKLITE, other diners are watching. KRACKLITE slaps the BOY across the face with the back of his hand.

KRACKLITE: You're determined to catch me out – aren't you? Answer me!

The BOY stares bewilderedly at KRACKLITE – tears well up in his eyes, but he doesn't cry out. His MOTHER is now shouting.

MOTHER: (*In Italian*) Do all Americans behave like this?

KRACKLITE: (*To the* BOY) What is she saying?

BOY: She says that you are to sit down.

KRACKLITE: Your son is too damn beautiful! I might have had a son as beautiful as him! Where the hell is Ventimiglia anyway? . . . in the back of beyond somewhere? . . . a graveyard for has-beens – for mediocre has-beens. Show me where it is on a map . . .

MOTHER: (*In Italian*) You leave my child alone – what are you, some sort of child-molester?

KRACKLITE: What does she say?

BOY: (*Speaking steadily*) She says do you kidnap children?

KRACKLITE: (*To the* MOTHER) No . . . it's worse than that, woman – much worse.

He lets the BOY go, two other diners are approaching the table – the BOY plucks at KRACKLITE's sleeve, KRACKLITE wrenches his arm away.

KRACKLITE: Don't touch me! How dare you touch me! What the hell do you think you are, some goddamn angel?

KRACKLITE is now weeping. Silently, the BOY takes – one after the other – four small onions out of his trouser pocket. He places them in a line on the white tablecloth in front of KRACKLITE. KRACKLITE stares, wondering what the BOY is doing – then he realizes the significance of the onions. He turns his head away.

KRACKLITE: (*Quietly*) Just because you're eight years old and your father's buried in some provincial graveyard far from anywhere . . . you make me sick . . . (*He mumbles into silence – ashamed.*)

KRACKLITE wrenches himself away from the two diners and the waiter who have come to restrain him. He looks ferocious – enough for them to hesitate before apprehending him. He stumbles out of the restaurant towards the road and, with the traffic hooting at him, crosses it in the direction of the Victor Emanuel Building.

Section Thirty-seven: Late Evening, Tuesday, 11 February 1986

SCENE 55: PANTHEON: THE EVENING BEFORE THE OPENING OF THE EXHIBITION

It's night time and the Pantheon is floodlit – it is framed exactly as it was before. The camera repeats the backward track as before. KRACKLITE is seen drunkenly drinking from the basin of the fountain. He stands up – his face dripping with water. He follows the retreating camera to the restaurant.

The restaurant is full of diners. There are bright lights, many waiters, a great deal of chatter and – a VIOLINIST. The same VIOLINIST KRACKLITE met in the Concert Hall toilets. His red violin case is on a chair.

KRACKLITE, taking bites out of a messy, half-eaten pizza, stares over the low privet hedge (in tubs) at the bright lights and chatter. He recognizes the VIOLINIST – who is serenading the diners with the same tune we heard him play before.

KRACKLITE exchanges a look of recognition with the VIOLINIST – who acknowledges him with a smile and a familiar nod. He doesn't stop playing.

KRACKLITE walks in among the diners, brusquely bumping into waiters and jogging the elbows of diners. The VIOLINIST keeps playing.

KRACKLITE has attracted attention. He is being stared at – he takes immediate dislike to a middle-aged woman eating figs.

KRACKLITE: I shouldn't eat those figs, lady, they're an aphrodisiac and I don't think you'd be up to it . . .
(*The woman calls to a waiter.*)
Calling him won't help . . .
(KRACKLITE *tries to sit down on an empty chair.*)
Can I join you? . . . My wife always wanted to eat in company . . .
(KRACKLITE'*s clumsiness sends cutlery flying.*)
I like eating in company too . . . I'm just like you really . . . I've got exactly the same metabolism as you have . . . the trouble is . . . (*Leans forward to a young woman seated at the next table*) I'm very interested in bellies . . . Do you have a belly? . . .

The woman's escort seizes KRACKLITE by the messy lapel and says something in Italian. He gets up and plates and flowers crash to the floor.

KRACKLITE: Here's mine . . . (*Lifts his shirt out of his trousers.*) A little larger than yours perhaps . . . (*Strokes his stomach*) because . . . do you know why . . . because it's rotting away from the inside. Everything I eat . . . I throw up . . .
(*Another table goes over, waiters appear from all sides.*)
Here, lady, feel it . . .
(*He grabs a woman's arm and forcibly makes her stroke his naked stomach.*)
Don't be frightened . . . it won't bite you . . . It's only biting me . . .

KRACKLITE's trousers begin to slip, a man grabs his collar, KRACKLITE struggles free, and pushing aside chairs and diners, makes for the exit on to the square, he turns to face his pursuers.

KRACKLITE: Do you know, I'm sure Jesus Christ himself would have died of stomach cancer if he hadn't been crucified first . . .

The bells of the surrounding churches begin to strike and peal for midnight. They immediately begin to remind the drunken and exhausted KRACKLITE of his first night in Rome at the same restaurant where he was celebrating his birthday. He listens and remembers the route around the Pantheon and he remembers applauding the Pantheon.

Pursued by three waiters and two diners, KRACKLITE pushes through the row of privet bushes in tubs, and runs into the Pantheon Square. Clutching his trousers, he runs down the street beside the Pantheon – he is now chased by other onlookers. Surprisingly, for his age, weight and condition, he runs fast – supported by alcohol and adrenalin.

There now follows a chase around the Pantheon that mocks the first time it happened. In and out of the artificial lights, with long shadows racing first ahead and then behind. The clatter of running footsteps, shouts, dogs barking. Once or twice, a pursuer catches up with him, to be punched or thrown off by KRACKLITE.

As he runs back into the Square, the bells of all the neighbouring churches continue to ring.

KRACKLITE completes the circle round the Pantheon. When he ends up in front – where the group met before to applaud the building – KRACKLITE falls/trips into an exhausted heap at the feet of diners from the restaurant, waiters and police. There is the sound of police sirens in the distance. Dirty, his trousers ripped, his face red and sweating, he lies on his back, convulsed, in pain, laughing and weeping. As his pursuers circle curiously around him, KRACKLITE enthusiastically claps and applauds the Pantheon.

Section Thirty-eight: Early Morning, Wednesday, 12 February 1986

SCENE 56: POLICE STATION

Early in the morning, KRACKLITE – dishevelled, clothes awry, dirty-faced – is ushered – quite tenderly – into a palatial police station. There are marble floors, mahogany desks, imposing

statues, echoic voices, shafts of low sunlight. KRACKLITE's shoelaces are undone – he carries his jacket.
He is led across a large echoing hall to a row of chairs – and asked to sit down before a large desk covered in files and papers. He sits without resistance. A wide shot reveals him sitting underneath a large picture – Ribera's *Drunken Silenus* – a gloomy, grotesque, disturbing painting. Not far from him is a table covered in a black velvet cloth – on which are ranged, in neat rows, some forty marble noses. KRACKLITE sits and looks around him. A few chairs away is the man whom KRACKLITE met on the Palatine Hill – the man who chipped off noses. He is leaning forward on his knees, he looks up and sees KRACKLITE. He gives KRACKLITE a discreet wink. He then takes out a large dirty handkerchief and blows his nose.
After a whispered conversation between two officials who keep looking in KRACKLITE's direction, a door opens, and a large benign, authoritative figure comes out, confers briefly with the two whispering officials and then takes a seat behind the desk, looks straight at KRACKLITE, then takes down his particulars – the barest of particulars that act as a summation of KRACKLITE's life. It's the last time we hear KRACKLITE speak. Without over-stressing the point – this is KRACKLITE's meeting with the ultimate dispassionate official. It's the final roll-call.

OFFICIAL: Name?
KRACKLITE: Kracklite – Stourley.
OFFICIAL: Nationality?
KRACKLITE: American.
OFFICIAL: Place of birth?
KRACKLITE: Chicago.
OFFICIAL: Present address?
KRACKLITE: Rome.
OFFICIAL: Age next birthday?
KRACKLITE: I'm not having another birthday.
OFFICIAL: Pardon?
KRACKLITE: Fifty-five.
OFFICIAL: Married?
KRACKLITE: Yes.
OFFICIAL: Children?

KRACKLITE: Er – yes.
OFFICIAL: Occupation?
KRACKLITE: Architect.
OFFICIAL: That's all. Thank you. You may go.
KRACKLITE: Is that really all?
OFFICIAL: What else could there be?

KRACKLITE stares and slowly puts on his jacket. He wanders out into brilliant sunlight.

Section Thirty-nine: Afternoon, Wednesday, 12 February 1986

SCENE 57: VITTORIANO MODEL ROOM

In a side room with a view of the atrium, all those we have met in the early scenes of the film are waiting for the opening ceremonies to begin – CASPETTI, PASTARRI, MORI, JULIO, TRETTORIO, IO, FLAVIA. The room has large models of the Victor Emanuel. There are champagne bottles and glasses. IO is opening a parcel. Others are reading congratulatory telegrams. LOUISA and CASPASIAN enter. Everyone greets LOUISA – she is looking beautiful, very pregnant, and somewhat apprehensive. The men kiss her on the cheek.

LOUISA: I am sorry we're so late – it's my fault. I didn't feel so good. I nearly didn't come. Where's Kracklite?
IO: He hasn't shown up.
JULIO: I've phoned his apartment – he isn't there – they haven't seen him.
IO: Good Lord! Look at this!

All the time he has been talking, IO has been undoing his parcel – it's full of postcards of Rome – all stamped and franked in Rome – some a little dog-eared. He spills them out on the table. IO, CASPASIAN and JULIO, FLAVIA flick through them.

IO: They are all addressed to Boullée and are all signed Stourley Kracklite.
(*He picks up a letter.*)
LOUISA: (*To* MORI) You couldn't get me something to drink, could you?

(MORI *pours her some mineral water.*)
IO: It's from my ex-wife – she lives in Paris. She says . . . (*Reads*:) 'These postcards have been arriving at my flat for the past nine months.'
(*He looks at* LOUISA.)
FLAVIA: (*With a laugh*) Poor Stourley!
IO: (*Returning to the letter*) She says they have amused her for so long . . . she wants to know if we know who Stourley Kracklite is – because she would like to meet him.
JULIO: So, at this moment, would we!
CASPASIAN: (*Just a little nervously*) I don't think we should wait any longer . . .

SCENE 58: VITTORIANO SIDE ENTRANCE

Outside the front of the exhibition hall – at a small side entrance – 30 feet from the main entrance – a few onlookers, a policeman and the guard on the door watch proceedings – most of the celebrities have entered – Caspasian's distinctive car is parked outside the front entrance.
KRACKLITE – looking calm and pale but shaven, with a pressed suit and a clean shirt, neat tie and shiny shoes – carrying his jacket – approaches through the parked cars and conceals himself behind a hedge – looking over to see if there is anyone who could recognize him.
He watches as FREDERICO arrives on his motorbike – carrying on the pannier a box we've seen before – it contains the silver scissors to cut the tape to open the exhibition. FREDERICO parks by Caspasian's car and enters the building by the main entrance – showing his pass to the doorman.
After FREDERICO has gone inside, KRACKLITE walks up to the side entrance and with assumed nonchalance, walks in. He is stopped. The doorman, employed for the occasion and not recognizing KRACKLITE, asks for KRACKLITE's pass or invitation. KRACKLITE – now knowing the system and what is required – hands him a wad of notes – it's not enough – KRACKLITE hands him some more – emptying his pockets. The man counts through the notes and he finds an English pound note. Smiling, he hands the English note back to KRACKLITE.

KRACKLITE with the slightest of smiles takes it. The doorman smiles, stands aside and KRACKLITE enters.

SCENE 59: VITTORIANO MODEL ROOM

Back inside the exhibition anteroom.

IO: Louisa – it doesn't look as though Kracklite's coming.

LOUISA: Can I have another drink? Something stronger.

(CASPASIAN *pours her a glass of wine and she drinks it very quickly.*)

IO: (*To* LOUISA) Whatever else has happened – this was always Kracklite's exhibition. Could you find a way to help us and open it on his behalf?

LOUISA: Why don't we let Caspasian do it?

(CASPASIAN *looks eager to accept but* IO *promptly steps in.*)

IO: It is most appropriate that you should do it – for Kracklite and for us.

FREDERICO enters carrying the box we saw him take off the motorbike. He opens the lid and takes out a pair of large silver scissors.

FREDERICO: (*Holding up the scissors*) Then let's get started.

LOUISA: If Kracklite appears . . . (*with a nervous laugh*) I'm quietly disappearing into the shadows. I'm in no mood for a confrontation.

(*She places a hand on her very pregnant belly.*)

CASPETTI: We are delighted, Signora Kracklite, that you have agreed to do this for us.

PASTARRI: (*Gallantly*) We can continue to benefit from the prestige . . . of an American celebrity.

CASPASIAN: (*Aside*) Without the embarrassment . . .

FREDERICO: (*In a whisper*) . . . of her clown of a husband.

They begin to move out into the crowd of celebrity guests in the atrium and climb the stairs. There is a wave of clapping as they walk through.

SCENE 60: VITTORIANO STAIRS

KRACKLITE walks through service corridors and climbs a back staircase in the gloom – away from the celebrations. Climbing many steps exhausts him.

SCENE 61: VITTORIANO EXHIBITION HALL

Inside the exhibition hall – the 'Louisa' party is climbing the staircase. It is shadowy – lit by braziers which give off white smoke. The crowd is illuminated by the Newton globes carried in the hand. LOUISA carries one. It illuminates her face – which shows a mixture of delight and apprehension. She leans on CASPASIAN's arm. CASPASIAN is busy talking to a journalist. The Boullée exhibits dwarf them all.

SCENE 62: VITTORIANO COLONNADE

KRACKLITE emerges from a dark staircase on to the brilliantly lit exterior of the Vittoriano – on to the colonnade. He avoids two carpenters – at work on the last detail – in case they recognize him. KRACKLITE walks along the colonnade – looking out over Rome where a series of 'Canaletto' boxes have been set up. He looks in the 'Pantheon Box' – a framing device to isolate part of the huge panorama of Rome.

SCENE 63: VITTORIANO MAIN HALL

Back inside the building, the party enters the Newton Room. A wide shot gives a panoramic view of the two halves of the spherical Newton Memorial and the surrounding exhibits – lit dramatically. Up on the balcony sunlight streams in through the balcony window. Ranks of assembled audience await the opening ceremony. CASPASIAN takes his place before a microphone and the celebrity party take their seats – on a row of chairs – again reminiscent of that row of chairs in the Piazza of the Pantheon and the Concert – with the same order as before, with KRACKLITE's seat noticeably empty.

SCENE 64: VITTORIANO COLONNADE

Up on the colonnade – out in the sunshine – KRACKLITE has reached the south terrace with the truncated cone and the top of the Boullée Newton Memorial whose huge substance is secreted inside the building.

SCENE 65: VITTORIANO MAIN HALL

Inside the building, CASPASIAN's speech is in Italian and is being translated simultaneously into English by a man whispering into a microphone for the purposes of English-speaking reporters who are standing huddled around him. The speech is full of florid references to Boullée, the Roman origins of European architecture, Piranesi, the problems of Modern Architecture, etc. Before the group of celebrities is the Grand Model of the Newton Memorial fronted with a generously wide, looped silk ribbon. Printed on the ribbon, as on the cake at the Pantheon building at the start of the film are the words: 1728–1799 ETIENNE-LOUIS BOULLÉE. LOUISA looks flushed and she is gripping the edge of her chair.

TRANSLATOR: Ladies and Gentlemen, honoured guests – Architecture in the Western world is in ferment . . . and it is the responsibility of *contemporary* architects to be seriously concerned. The very role of the architect itself is changing – possibly out of all recognition.

We have seen that the public over the last few years has developed strong opinions about the roles and purposes of architecture and has every intention of entering the debate. In their search for an architecture that avoids the excesses of utility and function, architects are searching for new inspiration. They are looking for new ways to use the examples of the Past. In Etienne-Louis Boullée they have found an excellent example.

Through him the continuity of the architectural vision that blossomed in Greece and Rome was transformed by contact with the democratic freedoms of the French Revolution. This exhibition – which confirms the visionary spirit of Boullée's contribution to Architecture – has come about because of the dedication of another architect – one of Boullée's most fervent twentieth-century admirers.

Boullée reserved his greatest inspiration for a Memorial he dedicated to Sir Isaac Newton, the English physicist whose optical, astronomical and mathematical theories became the root of Modern Science and the source of inspiration – not only to Scientists but also to Artists and Dreamers. This Memorial to Sir Isaac Newton is represented here today – at one two-thousandth of its original intended size – as the centrepiece of our Exhibition.

Way up above the hall, in a wide shot – KRACKLITE emerges on the balcony – backed by the balcony window. He stands and watches the ceremony – his attention largely on LOUISA. He notices she looks disturbed. She whispers to IO who looks concerned and holds her hand.

CASPASIAN is coming to the end of his speech of welcome.

CASPASIAN: . . . and so it is with great delight that, on Boullée's birthday, I ask Signora Kracklite to declare this magnificent exhibition open.

He takes the pair of silver scissors from a cushion proffered by FREDERICO. The orchestra plays. LOUISA gets unsteadily to her feet and takes the sharp scissors that sparkle in the light. She stands very pregnant in front of the large Dome of Boullée's Newton Memorial. The TV crew and the photographers are ready to film. At a signal from CASPASIAN, the gallery lights are dimmed and a spotlight picks out LOUISA – the scissors shine extra bright. She steps forward and speaks her carefully rehearsed opening speech in Italian. It is translated by the English translator. KRACKLITE watches dispassionately.

LOUISA: It is with great pleasure that I declare this exhibition open and hope it will bring many people to know and understand more of the work of Etienne-Louis Boullée, the great visionary architect who owed so much to Rome . . .

While LOUISA speaks, KRACKLITE – up on his balcony by the fan window – ceremoniously empties his pockets – keys, coins, watch, pens, wallet. He lays them neatly on a glass-topped exhibit – the activity is entirely reminiscent of what he did in an earlier bedroom scene. He lays down the one-pound note. He (and we) look closely at Newton's face and the apple blossom – symbol of gravity. KRACKLITE smiles and picks up the note again.

LOUISA cuts the tape, the ribbon falls off the Dome, the two halves of the enormous sphere close with a slam concealing the Newton 'gyrosphere'. The lighting of the Newton Room is reversed – the large space is brilliantly lit.

The audience applauds. The photographers flash, the orchestra plays . . . and LOUISA collapses. She is immediately surrounded. LOUISA goes into childbirth. The officials try to push the persistent photographers away. The scene is very reminiscent of

the crowd around BATTISTINO having his fake heart attack. KRACKLITE watches the proceedings from the balcony. He backs slowly towards the large fan window – tests its vulnerability with his hand, then leans his weight against it. It vibrates. He pushes hard.
Before the large illuminated Dome of the Newton Memorial, LOUISA gives birth. A baby is heard crying. A flushed LOUISA is glimpsed through the mêlée of bodies. The baby is held up – it's a boy – and is seen silhouetted against the Dome, now illuminated to represent 'noon'.
On the balcony, KRACKLITE eases the fan window from its frame. Calm and determined, he gives the final push. In a shower of glass and wood splinters – he falls backwards out into the late-afternoon Rome sunlight. There is a silence. The camera contemplates the open sky. The soundtrack hears the crying of a baby.

Section Forty: Afternoon, Wednesday, 12 February 1986

SCENE 66: VITTORIANO SIDE ENTRANCE AND PIAZZA DE VENEZIA
Outside, KRACKLITE has fallen on to the slope of the huge Boullée model of the truncated pyramid and broken his neck. His body has slid down the angle of the pyramid leaving a blood trail. Part of the window has snagged on the slope – the other half has fallen to the pavement. The corpse has come to rest on the roof of CASPASIAN's car, outside the entrance door of the exhibition. The car roof has gently buckled and KRACKLITE is cradled in the metal like a child in a cot. His shirt-tails are free – his stomach is naked. A close-up shows the pound note clasped in his hand – the apple blossom – Newton's symbol of gravity – revealed.
There now begins a tracking-reversing crane-shot. From across the road outside the entrance – with KRACKLITE's dead body as its initial centre, the camera backs away. The afternoon Roman traffic is revealed, the crowds around the entrance are revealed, and more and more of the Victor Emanuel Building is revealed. The Basilica is revealed . . . and the Campidoglio. Ambulances

arrive. The camera continues to back away, revealing the Piazza de Venezia and frontage of the Victor Emanuel. The building is surrounded by the Roman rush hour. The streets are full of noisy traffic. The camera continues to back away and eventually settles on the eight-year-old BOY seated on a stone bench playing with his gyroscope. The camera moves into the gyroscope. The gyroscope in close-up spins round and round, its axis becoming more and more diagonal – until – this machine that can temporarily withstand gravity – collapses. Cut to black.

'Dear Boullée'

Kracklite sent these postcards to an address in Paris where he believed that Boullée had spent his last months. Sometimes the postcards were sent daily, sometimes, in moments of crisis or euphoria, he sent as many as six a day. In times of despair or ennui, there were long breaks in the correspondence. One hundred and twenty-four of these postcards are printed here in chronological order. It is hoped shortly to present this postcard correspondence as a short film called *Dear Boullée* which will complement *The Belly of an Architect*.

I

Piazza del Popolo

Wednesday
29th May 1985

Monsieur Boullée,
I hope you don't mind me writing to you like this. I feel I know you well enough to talk to you. I think my wife is poisoning me! I'm sure it's part of her general animosity towards you – you can laugh but I'm serious.

Yours, with respect,
ST. KRACKLITE
(Architect)

2

Piazza del Popolo

Friday
31st May 1985

Dear Boullée,
Do you know of any architects who have been poisoned? Could Bernini have hated Borromini enough to have poisoned him? Maybe Corbusier should have been poisoned and not drowned. Maybe that's what happened. What was Corbusier's favourite drink? He drank a glass of poisoned acqua minerale, went swimming and sank. The pathologist was in the conspiracy and gave a verdict of death by drowning. What do you think?

With respect,
STOURLEY KRACKLITE
(Architect)

3

Piazza del Popolo

Saturday
1st June 1985

Dear Boullée,
They tell me you never got married. Is it an impertinence to ask you why? I've been married seven years. Her name is Louisa. Her father is an Italian – Carlo Boldoni. The Italians are masters of poisoning, aren't they? Sigismondo Malatesta, Amerigo Sforza, Lucretia Borgia – why not Louisa Boldoni? Maybe it was her father's idea that she should poison me. What could they achieve by doing that?

Yours, with respect,
S. KRACKLITE

4

Piazza del Popolo

Monday
3rd June 1985

Dear Boullée,
The Romans had rooms for everything, didn't they? – for hot water, cold water, for warm water, for cool water, for vomiting and for fornicating, for keeping snakes, for examining the entrails of sheep – perhaps they had a room for poisoning husbands! I bet they built one in the Victor Emanuel Building. I need to find it and brick it up. Do you think I'm mad. . . ?

Yours with respect,
S. KRACKLITE

5

Piazza del Popolo

Tuesday
4th June 1985

Dear Boullée,
Went to a concert on the Campidoglio – and listened to Vivaldi surrounded by huge pointing fingers and giant feet. I had to leave. I met a violinist playing by himself in the toilet. He could never play in public because of the shits – his nerves went to his stomach. I've seen this violinist before somewhere. He keeps his violin in a red case. He knows all about you . . . and thinks Newton had a better brain than Einstein. He asked me if I had a nervous stomach. I had to reply – not before I came to Rome.

Yours,
ST. KRACKLITE

6

Piazza del Popolo

Wednesday
5th June 1985

Dear Etienne-Louis,
A fortnight ago on the train from Paris to Rome I met a film director who said he had once been a carpenter. I asked him if it had been a big jump. He said no. He still kept a sharpened pencil behind his ear and wore corduroy trousers. He plunged his hands in sawdust every night so that his wife could still enjoy the smell of wood. Her name was Mary. They were childless. Neither of them were happy. They were waiting for a miracle.

Yours,
STOURLEY KRACKLITE

7

Piazza del Popolo

Wednesday
5th June 1985
Noon

Dear Boullée,
Were you ever ill? They tell me you were wealthy – you could have afforded the best Parisian doctors. Were they any good? Do you think I should see a doctor? Or would going to the police be more sensible? Could you go to the Italian police and say, 'My wife is poisoning me'?

Yours,
STOURLEY KRACKLITE

8

Pantheon

Wednesday
5th June 1985
6.00 pm

Dear Boullée,
Why didn't you ever come to Rome? 1785 would have been a good year. No doubt there would have been cows in the Basilica Julio and 427 species of plants in the Colosseum. The Piazza di Rotonda would have been slimy with fish and offal – you would have to have looked at the Pantheon over a sea of fishwives. Still – seeing the real thing is better than looking at that charlatan Piranesi. He has a lot to answer for. All Europe, thanks to him, thought the Piazza Navona was a mile long.

With respect,
STOURLEY KRACKLITE

9

Pantheon

Thursday
6th June 1985

Dear Boullée,
I'm being made a prisoner of my own dream – they are saying that I can't do this – and permission will never be granted for that – and this is impossible and that is too difficult. They ask for meetings in which they squabble with one another and worry me with the price of postage stamps – yet spend hours eating on the exhibition finance budget. Perhaps this is no surprise to you.

Yours,
ST. KRACKLITE

10

Pantheon

Friday
7th June 1985

Dear Boullée,
The Romans need to exaggerate – ten superlatives are necessary to describe the mildest pleasure – that way words soon lose their effect – it's like a drug habit – each time a larger dose of superlatives is necessary. Cold turkey to a Roman must be tape across the mouth.

Yours, with respect,
STOURLEY KRACKLITE

11

Pantheon

Saturday
8th June 1985

Dear Boullée,
Did you know any Romans? They are charming and aggravating in equal measure – ever watchful to create a good impression – la bella figura. *Our hosts in Rome are the Specklers – they don't sound very Italian but there have been Speckler architects in Rome for six generations. Io is so polished he'd make chromium envious. He has a son, Caspasian, who is to be my chief assistant – he dresses like a movie star and speaks five languages – Louisa is very impressed. Our banker is a vulgar fat man called Caspetti. He sweats like a sprinkler in the shape of a toad. I'm glad to see that Io thinks him vulgar – Louisa thinks he's dangerous.*

Yours, with respect,
STOURLEY KRACKLITE

12

The Spanish Steps

Sunday
9th June 1985

Dear Boullée,
'Having a wonderful time – wish you were here' – isn't that what they write on the back of a picture postcard? Could I write that with any honesty? My mother used to write postcards – to my father's relations in Germany and that's what she always put – even though there was never any hot water and there were bugs in the bed and it continually rained and my father spent his time drinking and eating, whilst we drank tepid coffee and lived on doughnuts.

Come to think of it – that's what I eat and drink now.

Yours,
STOURLEY KRACKLITE

13

The Spanish Steps

Monday
10th June 1985

Dear Boullée,
I'm giving up drinking. I go to bed excited and wake up tired. I've photocopied and enlarged the stomach of an heroic statue of Augustus by stages until his navel is as large as my head.

Augustus didn't have any children that survived him, did he? I'm told his wife poisoned him. How curious to consider the heroic stomach of Augustus and imagine him poisoned.

Yours,
STOURLEY KRACKLITE

14

The Spanish Steps

Tuesday
11th June 1985

Dear Boullée,
It is said that the study of architecture is an excellent training for life – but lousy if you want to build buildings. You were sensible to train as a painter – that way you could at least avoid blocking out the sun.

Yours
ST. KRACKLITE

15

The Spanish Steps

Wednesday
12th June 1985

Dear Boullée,
My wife is learning Italian very quickly – she's learning to swear in Italian – the best I can do is add 'O' to the end of a word – could you speak in Latin? – if you can – see if you can translate this – I saw it scratched on a church wall next to a phallus fashioned like the leaning tower of Pisa . . . SIC FATUR LACRIMANS IMMITIQUE HABENAS.

Yours
STOURLEY KRACKLITE

16

The Spanish Steps

Thursday
13th June 1985

Dear Boullée,
We have an excellent venue for your exhibition – the Victor Emanuel Building right in the middle of Rome – right on the Capitoline Hill. The she-wolf suckled Romulus under my feet. It's a privilege – the building is also the Italian tomb to the Unknown Warrior – a monument to Death and Glory – would you have approved? The Romans call the building the typewriter or the wedding cake – it's shaped like a Remington and looks as though it's covered in icing sugar – a wedding typewriter. A tomb in the shape of a sugar-coated typewriter? A monument to honey-coated words. Rome is full of inscriptions. Do architecture and words complement one another?

Yours,
STOURLEY KRACKLITE

17

The Spanish Steps

Friday
14th June 1985

Dear Boullée,
I am always dreaming that I am climbing stairs. There are more stairs in Rome than on the Tower of Babel. There are two thousand on the Victor Emanuel – Caspasian says you were lame from syphilis and the building would have been your nightmare. Is this true? Caspasian is a gigolo – I bet he irons his underpants . . .

Yours,
STOURLEY KRACKLITE

18

Piazza Navona

Saturday
15th June 1985

Dear Boullée,
I am curious about the 'armilliary sphere' that you hang in the Memorial Building to Newton. Something similar also appears on the English pound note – along with a portrait of Sir Isaac Newton. I've lost mine. I usually carry one for good luck – a man who discovered gravity is a friend to architects – by fixing our feet on the ground he enabled us with equanimity to hold our heads in the clouds. Your armilliary sphere reminds me of a toy my father gave me – a gyroscope that danced steadily on a length of string – without falling – a veritable deterrent to the forces of gravity. And when it stopped spinning. . . ? When will I stop spinning?

Yours,
ST. KRACKLITE

19

Piazza Navona

Sunday
16th June 1985

Dear Boullée,
I wonder what you would have thought about the Victor Emanuel Building? I told them you'd approve. Your approval is important. Everything's on a huge scale. There's a bronze equestrian statue with testicles as big as watermelons – the eight bronze-casters had a meal in the horse's belly when they'd finished. They tell me the architect died of pneumonia. Pneumonia seems a strange disease to die of in Rome where everyone of importance is poisoned. At 6 o'clock each evening I vomit my last meal – it's as regular as clockwork. I've finally decided to see a doctor. I'm sure he thinks I'm faking.

Yours
STOURLEY KRACKLITE

20

Piazza Navona

Monday
17th June 1985

Dear Etienne-Louis,
A thought has occurred to me – can you understand English? Did America mean anything to you at all? If you admired Newton, you must have known something about English science.

I'm told that Diderot wrote to you. He was an Anglophile. Did you contribute anything to the French Encyclopedia? Would you have known Benjamin Franklin? Do I sound like a journalist?

Yours,
STOURLEY KRACKLITE

21

Piazza Navona

Tuesday
18th June 1985

Dear Etienne,
Today we have our first official planning meeting and progress is slow.

I saw Caspasian Speckler across the room – he was pointing and gesticulating like a gigolo on heat. When I was his age I was hard at work in an architect's office, not entertaining the glitterati, posing for the gossip cameras, and ogling other men's wives. The man is a pariah! Louisa, I can see, is impressed.

Yours,
STOURLEY KRACKLITE

22

Piazza Navona

Wednesday
19th June 1985

Dear Boullée,
I was sick today in public after trying so hard to hide it . . . outside the Stazione Termini – Flavia asked me if I was making some comment about the building. Flavia is a strange girl – she always carries a camera – a 1940s Leica – yet I rarely see her use it – maybe she thinks it's a costume accessory. Her father, Io, is very offhand with her – she is more talented than her wretched brother, Caspasian. I imagine Caspasian to be like Ledoux – shocking for the sake of it.

Yours, with respect,
STOURLEY KRACKLITE

23

Piazza Navona

Thursday
20th June 1985

Dear Boullée,
I've been to see a doctor. He seemed more interested in architecture than medicine – I'm taking pills – my head feels light, my pulse gallops and my urine is milky – still, I feel better . . . maybe it takes an architect to cure an architect. They tell me Sangallo was obsessed with his health – all his food was sieved and he never ate anything black.

With respect,
STOURLEY KRACKLITE

24

Castelangelo

Friday
21st June 1985

Dear Etienne-Louis,
Midsummer day. The shortest night. The Corso is full of people at 3 o'clock in the morning. Are they Romans or visitors? Most of the people working on the exhibition aren't Roman. They're from Venice or Naples or Sicily. I don't know if there is such a thing as a true Roman. I'm told they all come here for the film industry. Is putting on an exhibition a good substitute for making a film?

Yours,
STOURLEY KRACKLITE

25

Castelangelo

Saturday
22 June 1985

Dear Boullée,
I took Louisa to see the Piazza de Pigorria – the only building in Rome that looks as though it might possibly have been designed by you – in miniature. I do believe that if you had applied for Italian citizenship – it might have been granted – even if you had to wait for it until 1936. Louisa is impressed – though not favourably.

Yours, with respect,
STOURLEY KRACKLITE

26

Castelangelo

Tuesday
25th June 1985

Dear Boullée,
Your drawings from the Bibliothèque Nationale arrived today. I spent all day eagerly looking at them through a magnifying glass – I counted 700 men wearing cravats on the terraces of the opera house. I looked for your self-portrait – I think I found it. You are sitting on a stone bench outside the second entrance to the grand library. You're 3 millimetres high – its difficult to see if you're laughing.

Yours
ST. KRACKLITE

27

Castelangelo

Wednesday
26th June 1985

Dear Etienne-Louis,
By addressing you like that I hope you don't find me too familiar – I was writing to you yesterday and Louisa looked over my shoulder. I said I was writing to my father – a feeble reply which only alerted her suspicions because unlike you, he's been dead for 15 years. She thought I was being facetious and told me to keep my secrets to myself.

Yours,
ST. KRACKLITE

28

Castelangelo

Thursday
27th June 1985

Dear Boullée,
Today I have seen the final plans for the exhibition – you would be pleased. The itinerary proceeds from 3 triangles to 2 squares to a circle – 3 pyramids, 2 cubes and a sphere . . . and the source of light in the sphere – Newton's monument – is at the exact centre of the Vittoriano. Now we have to build it – and we have 8 months – is it enough?

Yours,
ST. KRACKLITE

29

Castelangelo

Friday
28th June 1985

Dear Boullée,
I visited England several times when I was a young man and my strongest impression was the colour green. Here in June there is no green – the sun has scorched it all away. The vegetation has taken on the colour of the Roman buildings. I was right to insist that there be no green in the exhibition. There will be no blue either. This is an exhibition of buildings – orange, brick red, white, yellow, cream, grey, red and black under the Roman sun. Do you approve?

Yours,
ST. KRACKLITE

30

Castelangelo

Saturday
29th June 1985

Dear Boullée,
The pains continue. I've taken to eating a great deal of fruit. Do you think that's a good idea? It must be easier to be a strict vegetarian in Rome than in Chicago. Were there vegetarians in Paris in the 1780s – not out of necessity but by choice? My turds are often the colour of coal and my breath is hot enough to burn paper.

Yours
STOURLEY KRACKLITE

31

Castelangelo

Monday
1st July 1985

Dear Etienne,
Louisa is getting to look like a Roman: her hair is shorter, her skin tanned.

The markings on her body from her underwear are as sharp-edged as though they were painted on. I pretend to be asleep and watch her through a gap in the sheet. She smiles as she undresses and has begun to read cheap Italian novels – in Italian – Caspasian's taste, I shouldn't wonder.

Yours,
STOURLEY KRACKLITE

32

Castelangelo

Saturday
6th July 1985

Dear Etienne,
The Castel St Angelo. Hadrian's tomb originally – much like Augustus' tomb – though that is now a neglected ruin. The doctor at the Colosseum reckoned Mussolini wanted to be buried there. Mussolini – despite his short stay – has left his mark everywhere. If he'd been murdered here, I suspect in 50 years it would be visited and pointed out with that peculiar brand of Roman pride at its obscenities.

Yours,
STOURLEY KRACKLITE

33

Castelangelo

Thursday
11th July 1985

Dear Boullée,
The Castelangelo Bridge. This is the bridge of the first recorded traffic jam. And the first time that traffic was kept to the right – I don't know which bridge the British took as a model. Dante in 1300 described the pilgrims going over this bridge to St Peter's. He was an outsider, exiled from Florence, reluctantly living in Rome. I am not here reluctantly, though I do feel like an exile in a foreign country.

Yours,
STOURLEY KRACKLITE

34

The Tiber

Monday
15th July 1985

Dear Boullée,
This morning I went blind for 10 minutes. I was sitting by the Tiber in the bright sun and felt giddy and then everything went white. I searched for my glasses, but it made no difference; I panicked for several minutes. Frightened I'd fall in the water. I called out, but the roar of the water drowned out anything.

Slowly, my sight came back. What sort of illness can I have?

Yours,
STOURLEY KRACKLITE

35

The Tiber and St Peter's

Tuesday
16th July 1985

Dear Etienne-Louis,
I have been given an office in the bowels of the Vittoriano – the local affectionate name for the Victor Emanuel Building. I sit surrounded by the plaster models of the Vittoriano Competition held back in the 1860s – massive dusty plaster heads of giant horses – huge models of buildings never realized. Were there ever models made of your Newton sphere and do they now lie covered in 200 years of dust in a subterranean vault somewhere, forgotten? – and will some of the architects in the future undertake an exhibition on Michael Graves or Richard Rodgers and sit among their models dreaming?

S. KRACKLITE

36

The Tiber and St Peter's

Friday
19th July 1985

Dear Etienne-Louis,
The colours of Rome are the colours of human flesh and hair – for the most part warm – orange, orange-red, browns; and warm whites – cream – then warm blacks. No blue and only the darkest of greens – an exaggerated point of view? What colours would your buildings be? I have grown so used to your drawings being in black and white – it's difficult for me to see them in any colour.

Yours,
STOURLEY KRACKLITE

37

St Peter's

Sunday
21st July 1985

Dear Boullée,
Julius Caesar's birthday. Were you a great correspondent – an indefatigable letter-writer? Who did you write to? Le Notre or Mansard or Bernini?

I read of Bernini's plans for a revision of the Louvre. How the Parisians courted him and laughed behind his back.

Who else could I write to? I'd write to Inigo Jones. He suffered from nose bleeds and was laughed at at court for his Welsh accent. I'd write to Brunelleschi in sympathy against those Florentines who couldn't believe he could put a dome on a cathedral. The paymasters never change – all talk and swagger – keen for status – they take the praise for success and leave failure for the architect.

Yours,
STOURLEY KRACKLITE

38

St Peter's

Friday
26th July 1985

Dear Boullée,
Nobody has a straight job here – a single occupation. Doctors are archaeologists, architects are gynaecologists, bankers are art historians, film producers sell ice-cream, linguists build greenhouses. What were you apart from an architect? – a campanologist – a grammarian – a maker of cannon-balls?

Yours,
STOURLEY KRACKLITE

39

St Peter's

Monday
29th July 1985
3.00 am

Dear Boullée,
I can't sleep – I'm writing this in the dark – so much for the doctors who think the body is a house – I spend more time squatting in the bathroom than I do lying in bed. I must eat less at night. Roman hospitality makes a dinner last three hours and six courses and is short on fibre. If I'm to live to your age, I must change my diet.

ST. KRACKLITE

40

St Peter's

Tuesday
30 July 1985

Dear Monsieur Boullée,
I now have the suspicion that these Italians want to put the exhibition on all by themselves. Suddenly everyone claims to know all about you – they are at last claiming you were God's gift to Architecture – one of them said this morning that you were Italian not French – all those years when they couldn't have cared less – I bet you're laughing!

Caspasian has already spent 400 million lire and there seems precious little to show for it.

If we intend opening on your birthday – as we must – we have barely six months to go.

Yours respectfully,
ST. KRACKLITE

41

St Peter's

Wednesday
31st July 1985
Midnight

Dear Etienne,
I have an assistant who dresses like a dandy – with a bow-tie and canvas trousers – he makes exceptional architectural models. I like him. He's an Anglophile. He is cheerful and bright, but indolent and misled by Caspasian. I lost my temper and punched him on the nose – no lack of blood. I regret it.

Yours,
STOURLEY KRACKLITE

42

St Peter's

Thursday
1st August 1985

Dear Boullée,
Today I went into the underground passages of the Caracalla baths . . . small stones fell from the roof and the ground is sodden. Mussolini rode his white horses down there in the dark. Maybe they were white through lack of sunshine. He had some of the tunnels blocked up – no one knows why. Perhaps he buried his architects down there. The scale and the atmosphere would have delighted you.

With respect,
ST. KRACKLITE

43

St Peter's

Thursday
1st August 1985
4.00 pm

Dear Boullée,
Garibaldi's shoe is supposed to be on exhibition in a glass case inside the Victor Emanuel Building – like Cinderella's. There is nothing personal of yours to exhibit – no writing desk, no discarded walking stick, no medals or silk hat – no wig or marriage certificate. Io asked me yesterday if, with this exhibition, we are inventing you in our own image. I have to confess he might be right.

ST. KRACKLITE

44

St Peter's

Thursday
1st August 1985
6.00 pm

Dear Etienne,
Three postcards on one day. I'm trying a new drug and can't stop writing. Did you ever have to deal with Robespierre? I have a Robespierre and a Danton and a Hébert and a Marat and a St-Just – they are all supposed to be on the same side, but are intent on decapitating one another. Sometimes I am cast as Louis XVI after his capture at Varennes – held in isolation and contempt, brought sandwiches in an underground office that resembles the Bastille.

Yours,
STOURLEY KRACKLITE

45

St Peter's

Thursday
1st August 1985
8.30 pm

Dear Boullée,
Four postcards on one day – still maybe it's Augustus' birthday. The pains are returning. I now feel stupid to think that Louisa might have been poisoning me. She could drown me instead – I can't swim. Can you swim? I wonder if you and I are at all alike? Is that presumptuous of me?

Yours,
ST. KRACKLITE

46

St Peter's

Thursday
1st August 1985
11.00 pm

Dear Boullée,
Five postcards in one day. In an autopsy, does the navel have any interior shape? Consider how important it was in the womb. Imagine making a collection of navels – keeping them in formaldehyde.

Augustus on all his statues has a navel shaped like a new moon. I wonder if that was anything to do with his predecessor's delivery by Caesarian section?

With respect,
ST. KRACKLITE

47

St Peter's

Thursday
1st August 1985
11.30 pm

Dear Etienne-Louis,
The Roman fountains never cease to be a surprise. Rounding a corner in narrow streets – and there is another one. When the water is turned off the sudden silence is remarkable.

I went to the Medici Palace last night, to a concert. They had lit the trees with coloured lights – they looked like models on an architectural table – coloured sponges on wire.

Yours,
STOURLEY KRACKLITE

48

St Peter's

Thursday
1st August 1985
Midnight

Dear Boullée,
Seven postcards on one day – a surfeit of postcards. Your unrelenting delight in symmetry can frighten people. They are afraid of your persistent point of view. If – when they look in a mirror – the left-hand side of their faces is unequal to the right – they panic or else hide their fear in suggesting you had little imagination and designed to a formula.

We all live to a formula. Maybe the secret lies in keeping that formula secret.

Yours,
STOURLEY KRACKLITE

49

St Peter's

Friday
2nd August 1985

Dear Etienne-Louis Boullée,
The Specklers took us to the Villa Adriana for a Roman picnic – 'déjeuner sur l'herbe', except that August thunderstorms kept rumbling over Tivoli. The pains are returning and I can't eat without vomiting.

If you breathe in and press your finger just to the right of your navel – can you feel a hard lump? Some days it's spherical, some days it feels like a cube. Most days it feels like a sharp-cornered pyramid.

I must have an old, old disease – did the Pharaohs suffer from stomach cramps? The Emperor Hadrian died of a perforated ulcer.

When you're 54 and grateful for being able to sleep at night and eat badly and pee like a fire-engine – what do you do if you suspect your wife no longer cares for your company? – sorry, Etienne – since you never had a wife – that was never your problem. Maybe you were a sensible man.

Yours, with respect,
STOURLEY KRACKLITE

50

St Peter's

Saturday
3rd August 1985

Dear Etienne-Louis Boullée,
I am apparently to be a father – were you ever a father?

If your wife is unfaithful how can you ever know the child is really yours? My belly aches again. I had grapes for breakfast – was that wise?

It could be that the child was conceived in Italy. How can you calculate the exact moment of conception? – you can't – what about the Catholic Church? I'm sure they would have a theological argument. In celebration of my good news – I have a plan for when you come to the christening of my new son. I will conduct you across Rome – on a journey – from postcard to postcard. There aren't many cities in the world where you can do that. You must congratulate me.

All the best,
Yours,
STOURLEY KRACKLITE

51

St Peter's

Sunday
4th August 1985

Dear Etienne,
Are architects known to be potent fathers? Which architects, to your knowledge, had the most children? What about Michelangelo? – not even a bastard? No, of course not. His women are men with breasts – not a good description of Louisa. If my son were to be French – I could call him Etienne-Louis – would you approve?

Yours,
STOURLEY KRACKLITE

52

St Peter's

Tuesday
6th August 1985

Dear Boullée,
I went to the Vittoriano late last night and had a shock. By accident or design the place looked like a Piranesi prison. All gloomy spaces – hanging chains and ropes – large ragged sheets looking like flags or shrouds.

Is Caspasian being ingenuous, or malicious, or provocative – or all three?

This may well be Caspetti's doing. A vulgar little man – all belly and money. Why do such people have all the power?

Yours,
STOURLEY KRACKLITE

53

St Peter's

Wednesday
7th August 1985

Dear Boullée,
Piranesi! All I hear is Piranesi. We have a meeting every Wednesday – they are sociable but I doubt their ability to make any progress. We talk about Pirandello and Sangallo and pasta and Orson Welles and philology and anything but the exhibition. Then Caspetti comes in unexpectedly – we all have to sit up and smile and listen to another interminable lecture on Piranesi.

Yours,
STOURLEY KRACKLITE

54

St Peter's

Thursday
8th August 1985

Dear Boullée,
Should a special category be made for 'architect/painters'? It would include Corbusier and Piranesi, and Canaletto – and yourself. At the head of the list would have to be Michelangelo. And for their enthusiasm for architecture – Andrea Mantegna and Piero della Francesca . . .

Perhaps it is too big a category to be valuable – like a special category for birds that have feathers. . . ?

Yours,
STOURLEY KRACKLITE

55

St Peter's

Thursday
8th August 1985
11 pm

Dear Boullée,
Did you spend hours watching your wife sleeping? Of course, you never had a wife – did you ever watch a woman you cared about sleeping? Louisa constantly smiles in her sleep – what's she dreaming about? Occasionally she farts. I'm not sure which is the more stimulating – a roguish smile or a puff of hydrogen sulphide.

Yours
ST. KRACKLITE

56

St Peter's

Friday
9 August 1985

Dear Boullée,
I took Louisa to the cinema to see my favourite film. I've seen it at least 30 times over 30 years. It's full of an appreciation of architecture. Although it was stupidly dubbed into Italian, it made me both invigorated and relaxed – my stomach pains vanished – I fell asleep in the third reel. Louisa shouted at me afterwards. I know why I married her but she obviously doesn't know why she married me.

Yours
ST. KRACKLITE

57

St Peter's

Saturday
10th August 1985

Dear Etienne,
I'm curious about Ledoux. What was he to you? Every architect now champions Ledoux – knows the location of his every wretched ruined chimney-piece and would treasure his nail parings.

Whereas in comparison, they pay you lip service and look blank when I ask them if they know your building in the Rue de la Ville-l'Eveque. I have no pupils, I just have a wife. I suppose that's one over on you!

Yours,
ST. KRACKLITE

58

St Peter's

Sunday
11th August 1985

Dear Boullée,
There are plans here in Rome to raze the Victor Emanuel Building to the ground. They say that when the foundations of the Vittoriano are lifted, the old Roman columns will spring up like blades of grass left under a plank of wood. They'll be white and etiolated for a few days and then after a week in the sun, they'll look as though they've never been hidden.

Yours,
STOURLEY KRACKLITE

59

St Peter's

Monday
12th August 1985

Dear Etienne,
I steal the stamps from the office – that's why they're always such small denominations. Strangely, I feel better – light-headed – my wrists and ankles ache, but my digestion is fine. I've started to take lazy walks. I've even started thinking about buying a bike. I am going to get to know Rome really well, so that I can take my son around and teach him its history with some real authority.

Yours,
STOURLEY KRACKLITE

60

St Peter's

Tuesday
13th August 1985

Dear Boullée,
I saw the celebrated model of ancient Rome today at the Roma Museum – it's covered in dust and periodically glass falls from the roof. I was taken around by a curator with a built-up shoe. He walked at the same pace all the time – his uneven footfalls echoing in the huge halls. Were you lame?

Yours,
ST. KRACKLITE

61

St Peter's

Thursday
15th August 1985

Dear Boullée,
Did you know that Sir Isaac Newton spent the last ten years of his life trying to reconstruct Solomon's temple at Jerusalem? A physicist who ends as an architect? – a religious architect at that. If you had lived longer what would you have become?
If I live longer what will I become?

Yours,
ST. KRACKLITE

62

Trevi Fountains

Friday
16th August 1985

Dear Etienne,
What did you feel about competition? Are you a good competitor? When Paris was full of fêted architects and the fashion was against you – how did you cope? Did you bite your lip and smile pleasantly or did you speak out so that the critics cried, 'sour grapes!' and your friends quietly congratulated themselves on warning you against yourself? Tell me.

Yours,
ST. KRACKLITE

63

Trevi Fountains

Saturday evening
17th August 1985

Dear Etienne-Louis,
I walked up and down the Vittoriano colonnade at sunset. I still cannot tire of the views of Rome from there. A good point is the North Terrace where the marble walls are pitted and a bronze balustrade is gouged and scratched. A discreet notice says it was the work of enemy bombs and shrapnel. I imagine if you had built the Newton Memorial outside Paris . . . it would have undoubtedly shown the violence of 1870 and 1914 and 1942 and 1945 – even 1968! Consider building a vast cube of stone merely to register the effects of violence – marked and dated as an indictment.

Yours,
STOURLEY KRACKLITE

64

Trevi Fountains

Sunday
18th August 1985

Dear Etienne-Louis,
I have been back to the Villa Adriana. Last time I was too ill and too upset to see it properly. It is beautiful. Hadrian continues to grow in my estimation. Was he truly an architect, or merely an architectural patron? His ideas for the Villa Adriana were more than a traveller's whim. Io tells me that Renaissance architecture started at the Villa Adriana. I can believe him.

Yours,
STOURLEY KRACKLITE

65

Trevi Fountains

Monday
19th August 1985

Dear Etienne,
A large Zeppelin slowly travels across the sky in Rome each day.
Rome has been used by tourists for two thousand years or more – and has, in turn, used them: fleecing them; telling them lies to amuse them; turning on the Roman charm and then the indifference.
A large Zeppelin travelling over St Peter's every day is not going to turn a head.

Yours,
STOURLEY KRACKLITE

66

Campidoglio

Tuesday
20th August 1985

Dear Etienne,
I'm determined to get fit again. For 3 mornings now I've run up and down the steps of the Ara Ceoli. If I finish at the top I can get my breath back staring at the view; if I finish at the bottom, I can get a drink at the breasts of a stone lion – a fountain at the bottom of the Campidoglio steps. View or water?

Yours,
STOURLEY KRACKLITE

67

Campidoglio

Tuesday
20th August 1985
8.00 pm

Dear Boullée,
I am losing Louisa – I am sure of it. She is a stranger to me. Everything is different – her manner, her clothing, her underwear, the way she plucks her eyebrows, her confidence – her contempt.

KRACKLITE

68

Campidoglio

Wednesday
21st August 1985

Dear Etienne,
The temperature and humidity in the underground rooms of the Vittoriano are like a winter in New England. When you cross out into the sun of the Piazza Venezia – you can mark exactly the Equator line – within seconds the sweat is pouring off me and I stink like a rat.

ST. KRACKLITE

69

Forum

Thursday
22nd August 1985

Dear Etienne-Louis,
I wonder why you never came to Rome? Did travelling make you ill? Were you suspicious of foreigners? Did you ever come to Rome? Did you ever eat an orange? Do you know what Vitamin C can do for you? It's supposed to make you healthy.

Etienne-Louis – what was the current stomach complaint when you were alive? – gallstones, kidney stones? Excess bile? Pancreatic carcinoma . . . ? . . . or is that a pasta eaten at Bolzano?

Yours, with respect
ST. KRACKLITE

70

Forum

Thursday
22nd August 1985
Midnight

Dear Etienne-Louis,
I think I've sent you this postcard before – and when I did – I didn't fear what I fear now – Louisa is being very stupid – more I cannot bring myself to say.

Yours,
STOURLEY KRACKLITE

71

Forum

Sunday
25th August 1985

Dear Etienne-Louis,
It's three days since I've written. I've slept for most of the time – and when I'm awake, I stare at the ceiling. The traffic goes around the Piazza Venezia all day – flickering on the ceiling. The bath has a dripping tap – and when there's a breeze, the windows rattle. You see the limit of my interest.

Yours,
STOURLEY KRACKLITE

72

Forum

Wednesday
28th August 1985

Dear Etienne,
I went to the airport early this morning and sat in the spectators' gallery to watch the planes take off for Chicago. I confess I wept. It would be so easy to buy a ticket and take a plane – and fly home . . . Yet, what does 'home' represent? An empty home, with Louisa here. I need to buy a ticket to fly back five years. Then I might – possibly – find something to fly home for.

Yours,
STOURLEY KRACKLITE

73

Forum

Saturday
31st August 1985

Dear Boullée,
I suppose it all started at the picnic at Hadrian's Villa. That little picnic was devised by that little schemer Flavia – it now seems like a nightmare – then it seemed liked an alcoholic dream: there was thunder and vomit and a rabid dog, with Flavia like an over-dressed witch taking photographs with her little metal camera. I bet her tongue tastes of metal. I wonder what her brother Caspasian's tongue tastes of? I'm sure Louisa knows. It was Hadrian's fault. They say that the Villa Adriana is haunted by his grief for his boyfriend Antinous.

Yours,
STOURLEY KRACKLITE

74

Forum

Sunday
1st September 1985

Dear Etienne,
I went across to the Augusteum before dawn this morning. The city is quiet, but there is a vast amount of animal life. The stones were covered in red spiders and black ants; the lower sky with bats; and the upper sky with swifts. All disappeared 5 minutes after the sun rose – why was that? It was 7 o'clock before the traffic became noisy.

See you,
STOURLEY KRACKLITE

75

Forum

Thursday
5th September 1985

Dear Etienne,
It's supposed to get cooler in September, but I can't feel the difference. Since I was 17 I've sweated – but now I've only got to stand up and I'm in a sweat. Curiously, I've begun to sweat between the nose and the upper lip. I have a permanent wet moustache.

Yours, with respect,
STOURLEY KRACKLITE

76

Colosseum

Thursday
12th September 1985

Dear Boullée,
Mosquitoes go for my ear-lobes – nowhere else – I think it's because it's the only part of me that doesn't sweat. My left ear-lobe has swollen to the size of a crimson cherry. I've found something else that's curious – I've begun to sweat between my fingernails and fingers.

Yours,
STOURLEY KRACKLITE

77

Colosseum

Saturday
14th September 1985

Dear Etienne,
I've been to Florence for the day to talk to the D'Arc D'Oro – they're happy to design the poster for the exhibition. Afterwards, I went to the Uffizi – there is a room there for Mannerist paintings. Do you think we are now in a period of Mannerism?

There was a Mannerist painter who drank his own urine and lived till 90 . . . and another who slept with a leech on his neck . . . and another who contemplated making himself deaf by gunpowder in order to improve his sight.

Yours,
STOURLEY KRACKLITE

78

Colosseum

Tuesday
17th September 1985

Dear Etienne-Louis,
I've looked so long for a likeness of you that I've been convinced I have one. Were you really so young-looking at 54 or is it the sculptor's flattery? Were you nearly bald and did you really admire Hadrian? I have a suspicion you were a Mason. Is this true? Every intellectual of the 18th century was a Mason.

Yours,
ST. KRACKLITE

79

Colosseum

Thursday
19th September 1985

Dear Etienne,
It's hot – very hot. I go to the office in the Vittoriano to keep cool. There are innumerable places to hide. I suspect even the rats have forgotten about them. I can travel about the building in secret. I've found a disguised boiler room. The pipes are cold, the marble damp. I sleep there during the day. The staff think I am out inspecting buildings. I only return to the apartment for a bath.

Yours,
STOURLEY KRACKLITE

80

Colosseum

Friday
20th September 1985

Dear Boullée,
Beneath the inscription below the Vittoriano colonnade – is a rough-hewn, grey stone – a strange object amongst so much highly sculpted white marble – its purpose is not certain – if I ask I am sure to get a prosaic answer. I will believe it is a stone shat upon by Victor Emanuel's horse – or a fragment of the Tarquinian rock trodden on by geese . . . or the weaning-stone of Romulus and Remus . . . the stone has a partly erased inscription which is difficult to fathom.

Perhaps we can believe it is the real foundation stone of the Newton Memorial chipped from Stonehenge in England, touched by Sir Christopher Wren, blessed by Charles II, sat on by Louis XIV and bequeathed to you.

Yours,
STOURLEY KRACKLITE

81

Colosseum

Saturday
21st September 1985

Dear Etienne-Louis,
I met a man who collected noses – the stone noses of statues. I collect bellies. He knocked the noses off. I photograph bellies – seat of digestion and gestation . . . and cancer. Why did he collect noses? – two holes in the head – an accident of evolution. No poet waxed eloquent about nostrils. What about navels? Are nostrils and navels fit subject for poetry? Rome is a belly . . . the belly of the Western World.

Yours, with respect,
STOURLEY KRACKLITE

82

Colosseum

Sunday
22nd September 1985

Dear Boullée,
I spend most nights walking around Rome. Last night I climbed through the Palatine Gardens in the moonlight. There was a headless statue on the west corner. The grass at its base was a sea of cats – they stared at me as though I was a ghost. I looked towards the Colosseum and I was sure I could see the Newton Memorial behind the arch of Titus. Caspasian says you were anti-Semitic. Did you know St-Just?

Yours,
ST. KRACKLITE

83

Colosseum

Monday
23rd September 1985

Dear Boullée,
I'm restless, I've got to keep moving. Io took me to Bassano Romano to an old villa abandoned, wasted, left to quietly rot. In America it would become a national institution – here it's a damp embarrassment, a failure to survive an economic change. Outside there are 3 stone busts – all smashed in the mouth – one suffers from jaw cancer, one from cleft palate, one from gum disease. Julio says it was children at play with stones. Flavia says it was deliberate vandalism. Io says it was frost. I say it was melancholia of the mouth.

Yours,
ST. KRACKLITE

84

Colosseum

Wednesday
25th September 1985

Dear Boullée,
Did you ever take a holiday? Did you ever need to see somewhere different? Talk a different language? Be where no one else had been before? I can't imagine that *being the pastime of an 18th-century intellectual – did Rousseau and Voltaire take holidays?*

Io said I should go to Monte Argentario and I did. I sat on the beach under a large umbrella and felt hot and bored . . . and sick. I waded into the sea to vomit unnoticed.

Yours,
STOURLEY KRACKLITE

85

Colosseum

Saturday
28th September 1985

Dear Boullée,
I took Io's car two days ago – a Mercedes, green and sleek and cleaned twice weekly – and I spent two nights in the hills above Tarquinia. I lay on the roof of the car and watched the shooting stars – and then the dawn – and I thought about longevity and Newton and you – that both you and Newton should have come together, that Newton lived till he was 85 and you lived till you were 71. How long will I live?

I fell asleep and woke stiff and covered in insect bites, I vomited all over Io's sleek upholstery. The car stank of sickness and sweat all the way back to Rome.

Yours,
ST. KRACKLITE

86

Colosseum

Sunday
29th September 1985

Dear Boullée,
You Europeans have great faith in medicinal waters. Io took me to a bath where the water smelt of sulphur and coated your fingernails in white paste.

There were frescos on the walls and ceilings where all the members of the Roman Pantheon were watching the Fall of Phaeton – the downward plummet from the chariot of the sun into the earth. There is a look of panic on Phaeton's face as he sees the earth rising to meet him. His mouth is wide open. Did he break his back? Or crush his skull? Did his knees come up through his chest? A violent death after such – but quick. No slow death in a hospital bed.

Yours,
STOURLEY KRACKLITE

87

Colosseum

Monday
30th September 1985

Dear Boullée,
To explain what happened to the Etruscans, some say they were fatally exhausted as a race, by malaria. A thousand years of shivering attacks, fevers, depression and thunderous headaches wore them away – father by child by grandchild. All caused by a buzzing, whining insect that attacks you like a blood-filled helicopter in the night when you turn on the electric light and open the shutters. You see how even an illness can be romanticized.

Tuberculosis got the treatment: Keats, the Lady of the Camellias, the foggy dew and so on. We must make romantic literature out of cancer – can you imagine that?

Yours,
ST. KRACKLITE

88

Victor Emanuel Building

Wednesday
2nd October 1985

Dear Etienne-Louis,
I feel so tired and when I sleep I dream of staircases, steps, and ladders – always fearing I will fall off – and when I do finally plunge, I land always in a green field – my back broken – unable to move – not being able to close my eyes which are being burnt out by the blinding sun.

Yours,
STOURLEY KRACKLITE

89

Victor Emanuel Building

Sunday
6th October 1985

Dear Boullée,
I stay away from the apartment as often as I can. Sometimes I'd rather sleep anywhere but here. I sleep on a marble slab high up on the Vittoriano Colonnade – deliberately using the stone as a pillow. When my body is stretched out like a frozen corpse, I almost cease to feel the pain in my belly. Occasionally, a cool breeze runs the length of the pillars. I imagine huge banners wrought with your plans hanging the length of the building blowing in the wind.

Yours, with respect,
STOURLEY KRACKLITE

90

Victor Emanuel Building

Tuesday
3rd December 1985

Dear Etienne,
I don't like doctors. They always see you at a disadvantage – when they have pored over your private parts – smelt your breath – fingered your tongue – how can you talk with them as an equal?

Yours,
ST. KRACKLITE

91

Victor Emanuel Building

Wednesday
4th December 1985

Dear Etienne,
I've been for the examination and now I've got to be patient and wait. What do you do to calm your nerves? I sit in front of a mirror and pick my nose. I remember doing it as a small boy and being cuffed on the ear. I'm sure my son will do it . . . and his son . . . It's a disreputable habit – like farting in church.

Yours,
STOURLEY KRACKLITE

92

Victor Emanuel Building

Thursday
5th December 1985

Dear Etienne,
I was told – I suspect I begin every postcard to you with an 'I' – that the architect of the Victor Emanuel committed suicide. Looking at the imperfections I can see why. The builders got away with murder – it's beginning to slip and crack. The interior woodwork is very poor.

Yours,
STOURLEY KRACKLITE

93

Victor Emanuel Building

Friday
5th December 1985
Midnight

Dear Etienne,
I've learnt something else about Zucconi, the architect of the Victor Emanuel building. He committed suicide by jumping off a building – some say it was the Palace of Justice. He landed on his back and broke his spine. It's not true. I made it up.

Yours,
STOURLEY KRACKLITE

94

Victor Emanuel Building

Saturday
6th December 1985

Dear Etienne,
They've found my hiding place in the boiler room. They send spies down to make sure I'm all right. First they did it subtly – a boilerman checking the pipes – then a security man – then they got less cautious – a secretary looking for ink! I chased her and she's complained to Io.

Yours,
STOURLEY KRACKLITE

95

Victor Emanuel Building

Sunday
7th December 1985

Dear Etienne-Louis,
Let me tell you about Louisa. She's cut her hair short – she buys Roman lingerie – even her American accent is changing – it's the influence of the Specklers – and this wouldn't surprise you – Io Speckler is the worst protagonist. I don't believe he has a wife in Paris – and certainly not living at number 16 rue de la Ville-l'Évêque. I've never found out what he does. What does he do?

Yours,
ST. KRACKLITE

96

Victor Emanuel Building

Tuesday
9th December 1985

Dear Etienne,
I've been introduced to a painter of fake marble – I'm told he's not the best, but his skill at trompe-l'oeil is amazing. He can identify and reproduce 49 different varieties of Greek and Italian marble and tell you from which quarry each of them came. I asked him if he could fake happiness. He didn't understand.

Yours,
STOURLEY KRACKLITE

97

Victor Emanuel Building

Wednesday
10th December 1985

Dear Etienne,
The municipal authorities of Rome have decided to permit us to erect the Boullée pyramid outside the front entrance – a tomb entrance for a tomb. Admittedly it is only 1/500 of the intended size – but consider it as a beginning. I now have a plan which I dare not even admit.

Yours,
STOURLEY KRACKLITE

98

Victor Emanuel Building

Thursday
11th December 1985

Dear Etienne,
This exhibition is just a beginning – an introduction – a mere overture to what we can plan – I intend to found a Boullée Society that will reconstruct full-scale – around the world – 10 of your buildings. Financed by international money we will erect the buildings as you designed them – to scale and with all the relevant detail. We will institute a permanent office to your memory and start a research centre.

Yours,
STOURLEY KRACKLITE

99

Victor Emanuel Building

Friday
12th December 1985

Dear Etienne,
Lequeue is fashionable. A feeble visionary after you – what was he like? – I bet he was a jumped-up protégé like Caspasian. I want to find a patron before I inaugurate the Boullée Society – some architectural luminary whose sense and experience will polarize enthusiasm.

Yours,
STOURLEY KRACKLITE

100

Victor Emanuel Building

Saturday
13th December 1985

Dear Boullée,
When I've found the right patrons for the Boullée Society, I'll inaugurate the programme. I'll nominate the Governors and a Chairman. The main offices will be in Paris, of course, near the Maison Alexandre, rue de la Ville-l'Évêque.

Yours,
STOURLEY KRACKLITE

101

Victor Emanuel Building

Monday
15th December 1985

Dear Etienne,
The first true Boullée building must be erected in America – in Chicago – overlooking the lake. Which shall we concentrate on first? I suggest we keep the Newton Memorial until building number 10 and work up to it – in expectation – where would be the best place? In Rome? Maybe if the plans to raze the Victor Emanuel happen . . . ? Who knows?

Yours,
STOURLEY KRACKLITE

102

Victor Emanuel Building

Tuesday
16th December 1985

Dear Etienne,
My symptoms don't change, only the geography. I used to marvel at the workings of the human body – not any more – consider how clumsy it is – ephemeral, ageing, changing, distorting. The intestines seemed pushed into the stomach cavity anyhow – not neatly coiled and firmly fixed. When the belly's ripped, out they spew like bloated spaghetti pomodoro.

Yours,
ST. KRACKLITE

103

Victor Emanuel Building

Wednesday
17th December 1985

Dear Etienne,
Have you ever been up in an air balloon? Have you seen how the earth looks so small? Your Truncated Tower would rise above the clouds. It could be built outside the harbour at New York, visible for 80 miles. We now have techniques that would surprise you. We could build it lighter and taller than you could imagine.

Yours,
ST. KRACKLITE

104

Victor Emanuel Building

Friday
19th December 1985
4.00 pm

Dear Etienne-Louis,
Six days to Christmas. I can eat ice-cream. In America only children and old ladies eat ice-cream – in Italy everybody eats ice-cream. Pistachio is green and reminds me of figs. Fragola looks like cat-meat. Chocolate looks like tar. There is a purple ice-cream that looks like bruised flesh – the only one I can eat without revulsion – yet I feel like a cannibal.

Yours,
ST. KRACKLITE

105

Victor Emanuel Building

Saturday
20th December 1985

Dear Boullée,
I feel a little better – and can talk of things that don't touch me personally. I decided to look at Piranesi without flinching. I have to admit he is to be congratulated – along with Canaletto (another popularizer) – he created a view of Italy that has stuck: fictional, exaggerated, but accomplished enough to convince those who need to be convinced – which, I suppose, is all of us.

Your achievement is greater; you invented a whole world on paper – not just a fiction based on a real place. This exhibition will convince everyone.

Yours,
ST. KRACKLITE

106

Victor Emanuel Building

Wednesday
25th December 1985

Dear Boullée,
Christmas Day. I'm fasting – what did you do on Christmas Day? I cannot keep a clock or a watch. They stop on me. Why won't time stay peacefully on my wrist? Is time not interested in me any more because I am dying? If I had rats – they'd be leaving. Do fleas leave a dying dog?

Yours,
STOURLEY KRACKLITE

107

Victor Emanuel Building

Tuesday
26th December 1985

Dear Boullée,
As the population of the world increases, what of architecture? They say that there is one architect for every 75,000 people – where did they get that figure?

To my knowledge there are 32 architects living on Chicago's Lakeshore Drive. What of China and India and Mexico? Each man should be his own architect. If you were an Adobe Indian – think how discreet your architecture would be – but supposing you were a barber from Little Rock?

Yours,
STOURLEY KRACKLITE

108

Victor Emanuel Building

Saturday
28th December 1985

Dear Boullée,
I'm like Marat – I stay in the bath. He tried to keep his skin damp to save himself from his scratching fingernails. I stay underwater to drown the smell.

My palms smell of glue made from sheep gut – the sort I used to use to stick down the first pictures I saw of your drawings – cut-out newspaper photos from the Tribune advertising French week at the Metropolitan Museum, New York.

Yours, in respect of sheep-gut glue,
STOURLEY KRACKLITE

109

Victor Emanuel Building

Thursday
2nd January 1986

Dear Boullée,
A new year and I've lived till 1986. I was born in 1932 – the year that Roosevelt became President of the United States and Hitler came to power.

I have become obsessed with the smells of decay: a dustbin of maggots at the Campidoglio, an old woman on the Corso who sleeps on the pavement, the smell of the pissoir by the Spanish Steps, the dried excrement along the Tiber Embankment, the dustbin lorry at the Otello restaurant – yet – with disappointment I have to report that they all smell the same. Decay always, ultimately, smells the same – and I am now identified with it.

Yours,
STOURLEY KRACKLITE

110

Victor Emanuel Building

Sunday
5th January 1986

Dear Boullée,
Little democratic Flavia asked me where the toilets were in the Newton Memorial; where could you get an ice-cream to give to the children; how far away was the car-park. I might have added where was the sick room and could an ambulance come right up to the main entrance.

Could such egalitarian niceties have been part of the Baths of Caracalla and, of course, the answer would have to be 'yes'. Who would pay for your funeral monument? You could ask Caspetti – he'd pay for it if his name was on it in big enough letters.

Yours,
STOURLEY KRACKLITE

111

Victor Emanuel Building

Monday
6th January 1986

Dear Boullée,
I dream of staircases and of tunnels, and believe that my insides must be constructed of faulty architecture and cracked masonry like the Vittoriano or the Palace of Justice, or those suspended arches on the Colosseum – does a baker dream his insides are made of dough and currants, and if he's ill – of stale cake and rotting bread?

Yours,
STOURLEY KRACKLITE

112

Victor Emanuel Building

Thursday
9th January 1986

Dear Boullée,
At long last the interior of the Newton Memorial is being completed – there is talk of an opening ceremony where the two sides – the two hemispheres – come together like a clap of thunder. I'm not too excited about that – it smells of exhibitionism – what afterwards? Not unless we can make it truly relevant am I going to encourage it.

Yours,
STOURLEY KRACKLITE

113

Victor Emanuel Building

Saturday
11th January 1986

Dear Boullée,
The parts of the truncated tower have arrived – in 20 pieces. I followed it from the island in the Tiber where it was made. An articulated lorry slowly carried the pieces across the city – passing the Colosseum and the Forum in homage. It's impressive though only 14 metres high. To simulate its top platform being in the clouds, we plan to drift white smoke from it, illuminated from beneath.

Yours,
STOURLEY KRACKLITE

114

Victor Emanuel Building

Wednesday
15th January 1986

Dear Boullée,
The Bibliothèque Nationale has sent a custodian to the Vittoriano to see if our security is good enough. Suddenly because your drawings are in demand, they must have chains and red tape and burglar alarms and fire-proofing and sprinklers. I bet such precautions are not relevant in Paris.

Yours,
STOURLEY KRACKLITE

115

Victor Emanuel Building

Monday
20th January 1986

Dear Etienne-Louis,
I'm not drowning – literally – only figuratively. Today I've seen my past life flash before me – at least, the last nine months of it. Flavia has been taking photos of me all this time – watching my every move. Most of the time I never knew she was there – I never realized what she was doing. There are at least 20 photos of me vomiting – and a hundred of me looking tired, weary and sick – all pinned up on her studio wall, and underneath – marking time with my miserable deterioration – photos of Louisa – for the most part in the intimate company of Caspasian. I've rarely seen her looking so happy.

Yours,
STOURLEY KRACKLITE

116

Victor Emanuel Building

Monday
27th January 1986

Dear Etienne-Louis,
Have you ever heard of Andrea Doria? He was a sea-admiral with the Venetians. According to Flavia I look like him. She thinks he looks like me because he shows his fat stomach. That's not fair – he's not so fat. Would I pose for such a picture? He was about my age when he was painted. It's an idealized image and yet it's very vulnerable. The pose is practically identical with the pose of Augustus I've borrowed. Maybe there are only a certain number of poses.

Yours,
STOURLEY KRACKLITE

117

Victor Emanuel Building

Tuesday
28th January 1986

Dear Boullée,
There is a money problem. We are short – the currency exchange is blamed – so is some tax-shelter finance . . . but, as far as I can see – the Italians are over-anxious – I cannot decide whether this is malicious or merely sloppy. What could you have built for $750,000?

Yours,
ST. KRACKLITE

118

Vittoriano

Wednesday
29th January 1986

Dear Boullée,
There is a problem. My office has been cleared away and I'm now squeezed into the model room – wedged between 2 crumbling models of the Vittoriano. On one of them the statue of Victor Emanuel has been turned to face the colonnade away from Rome – facetiously? Who knows – it might well have been Zucconi's political joke.

Yours,
STOURLEY KRACKLITE

119

Victor Emanuel Building

Thursday
30th January 1986

Dear Boullée,
I've stolen a book of the anatomical engravings of Vesalius. Did you ever hear of him? His bodies are like complicated urban maps of the future. Do you think all anatomists are necrophiliacs? Louisa accused me of being a hypochondriac. Were you a hypochondriac?

With respect,
ST. KRACKLITE

120

Victor Emanuel Building

Friday
31st January 1986

Dear Boullée,
Imagine me putting on an exhibition of Piranesi in Chicago. That's what Caspetti suggested – then taking the exhibition on to Paris and then to Rome. How would you feel about that? I have an idea my stay here would be easier if I suggested the idea was possible. Would you think it disloyal?

Yours,
ST. KRACKLITE

121

Victor Emanuel Building

Saturday
1st February 1986

Dear Boullée,
Forget it. I'm ashamed to have mentioned Piranesi as an exchange. I must really be getting sick. Sickness saps at your confidence. To steady my hands in the morning I bang them on the radiator – a poor exchange. I'm beginning to barter everything – and you know why? – because I'm frightened of losing everything.

Yours,
STOURLEY KRACKLITE

122

Victor Emanuel Building

Wednesday
5th February 1986

Dear Etienne-Louis,
Well – the chains have snapped – the break is final. Louisa's left me. The wardrobe is full of her winter coats and the drawers are full of her shoes – but she's taken her underwear. I'm left with only the outer skins. What can I do? Claim the child by force? Rip it out and carry it back to Chicago? I can't separate drama from melodrama from picking my nose.

Yours,
STOURLEY KRACKLITE

123

Victor Emanuel Building

Sunday
9th February 1986

Dear Etienne-Louis,
If you came to Rome and you walked down the Corso – how would I recognize you? For sure – you won't be carrying a set-square and a plumb-line. How would you recognize me? I'm 54, large, broad-chested, fat-bellied. With grey curly hair – 6ft 3 and 210 pounds and I walk with a slight limp in my left leg – a football accident years ago – and when I'm tired – it shows. For you I wear a white suit and . . . what do they say? . . . carry a rolled newspaper . . . wear a red carnation – no – all that won't be necessary – you'll recognize me all right . . .

STOURLEY KRACKLITE

124

Victor Emanuel Building

Monday
10th February 1986

Dear Etienne-Louis,
It's no good Etienne – I'm ousted – kicked out of the exhibition I spent the last 10 years of my life planning. It's Caspasian's fault. He's run off with my wife, my child and our exhibition. But I've an idea – suppose you came to open the exhibition – why don't you come? How about that? That would show them. You could stay in my apartment – Louisa's not there any more – I don't sleep too well – but I'm sure we'd manage.

Yours,
ST. KRACKLITE
(Architect)